I0566602

SALVATION (Nashville Nights, #2)
Carlisle Queen & Mateo Butler

Letting go never felt so good.
Carlisle Queen is dying and no one knows it.
Burying the pain of losing her friends and her professional swimming career in a terrorist attack, America's former sweetheart dulls her pain with drugs, pills and parties. The bomb left her with more than nightmares; shrapnel is lodged in her back and inching closer to her spinal cord. When the doctors tell her paralysis is inevitable, she decides to take her own life rather than face a lifetime in a wheelchair.

Mateo Butler isn't anyone's hero.

Reeling from the death of his little sister and his own cowardice, he spends his nights partying and his days ignoring the medical school acceptance letters and his parents' concerned phone calls. Just a couple of months from graduation, he's facing a future filled with shame and regret. The last thing he needs is to meet the woman who compels him to be a better man.

Can they save each other?

When Carlisle and Mateo meet, the chemistry between them is combustible. They play, party and hide their true selves until one night turns their lust into something more... something real. As secrets are revealed and walls collapse, what they were and what they might become doesn't matter as much as who they are together. When the choice comes down to life or death, can love be their salvation?

SALVATION

BY

ROBIN COVINGTON

Letting Go Never Felt So Good

This book is a work of fiction. Names, characters, places, and incidents are the product of the author's imagination or are used fictitiously. Any resemblance to actual events, locales, or persons, living or dead, is coincidental.

Copyright © 2015 by Robin Covington d/b/a Burning Up the Sheets, LLC. All rights reserved, including the right to reproduce, distribute, or transmit in any form or by any means. For information regarding subsidiary rights, please contact the Publisher.

Burning Up the Sheets, LLC
23139 Laurel Way
Hollywood, MD 20636

Visit my website at www.robincovingtonromance.com.
Edited by Nicole Bailey at Proof Before You Publish, Inc.
Cover design by Sweet & Spicy Designs.
Formatting by Anessa Books

E-book ISBN: 978-0-9905432-3-7
Paperback ISBN: 978-0-9905432-5-1

Manufactured in the United States of America
First Edition May 2015

Dedication

For Nancy Weeks.
Thank your for your help, your open heart, and your friendship.

Chapter One

Carlisle

I taste blood.

Smoke and acrid dust swirl around me and I cough and heave and struggle to orient myself. I reach out trying to find him, searching for Aaron. He was just here.

The blood is warm on my tongue, on my chin and it dribbles out each time I try to scream. I reach out, desperate. The pain in my body like a thousand sharp knives piercing my skin, digging in deeper than I could have thought was possible. I push through it, dragging my body across the paved walkway a few inches until I find him. Aaron.

I'd know him anywhere. My lover. My best friend. The strength of his body, the long lines of his swimmer's frame. My fingers touch him, sliding off the wet and warm liquid on his skin. The smoke clears and I scream.

I wrench up in bed, my throat raw from the screams I know I tried to make in my sleep. My body is covered in sweat, hurting from the pain of muscles tensed in terror and the very real pain I've endured for the past eighteen months.

I would love for this to just be a nightmare. A figment of my overactive imagination, the product of eating too much spicy food or reading Stephen King novels before bed. Something I could change or explain away. That would be fucking sweet.

I throw off the covers, a shiver jolting through my body when the air-conditioned air hits my damp skin. I know better than to linger in bed when this happens or to let this dream roll around in my head for too long. I make a tentative attempt to stand and the pain shooting through my back and down my right leg reminds me with teeth-gritting clarity that the bombing wasn't a dream. I have the metallic shards embedded deep in my body to prove it—morbid souvenirs from a time that should have been the best day of my life.

I lower myself back to the bed, maneuvering through the exercises I learned in physical therapy to combat the morning pain that often followed in the wake of my nightmares. My body would go into full clench in my sleep and I'd stay like that for hours, sometimes waking with a sore jaw from having ground my teeth together for so long.

Two quick knocks on my door and my roommate sticks her head through the opening. Her long fall of jet-black hair is tied up in a loose ponytail and her porcelain skin makes Olivia Yee look like a Korean doll. She is tiny too, her barely five-feet frame looks Lilliputian when she stands next to my five-feet eight-inch length.

"Was it a bad one?" Livvy asks in the voice that takes everyone by surprise when they first hear it.

Truth be told, it was the voice that compelled me to interview her as a potential roommate in the first place. I didn't need someone to help me pay the rent; my endorsement money and the insurance payout after the bombing in the athlete's village guaranteed that I never had to work again but I didn't want to roll around in this place and listen to myself think. Months spent in my private room in a rehab facility had provided enough "me time" to make me sick of the voices in my head.

With her low, husky voice, I was expecting the real-time version of Jessica Rabbit to show up the day of the interview but I was in for a surprise when a woman strolled in dressed more like Amy on *The Big Bang Theory*. She informed me of five things within the first five minutes: 1) that she was a lesbian but I wasn't her type as she "really wasn't into gingers"; 2) she had a serious girlfriend who lived in New York City; 3) she didn't really follow sports but the medals were awesome; 4) she was very sorry I had been blown up; and 5) that she was a phone sex operator to make money to pay for school.

I immediately regretted that she wasn't into gingers and

the fact that I loved the peen because I fell in love with her on the spot.

"I'm sorry. Did I disturb your time with Ron?" I ask about one of her regulars while slowly easing up into a sitting position. Livvy doesn't offer to help me, she knows I'll ask if I need it. I do take the bottle of water she hands to me as she sits down on the bed. "Was I loud?"

"Nope. Ron finished early and I heard something when I walked by."

I glance at the clock. Ten forty-five at night. I'm not going back to sleep anytime soon. I'd been so exhausted earlier that I'd crashed shortly after wolfing down takeout Chinese in front of the TV but now I'm fully awake and will be for hours. Lucky for me, between the city of Nashville and living next to Nashville University, I can always find something to do.

"You want to go out?" I scoot over to the side of the bed and quickly add when she opens her mouth to make up some reason why she can't go out, "You have one more final in two days. Go out with me tonight." I pout. "You're leaving me soon to get regular booty in NYC. Go out with me now."

She shakes her head and raises her arms to the heavens as if asking for help. "Oh, the guilt trip is strong in this one!"

I ease up onto my feet and test out the level of cooperation my legs will give me tonight.

"What's your number tonight?" Livvy asks, watching me closely from her perch on the bed. "You've had a pretty good week, yeah?"

I nod and make my way around the end of my bed, pulling off my t-shirt and shorts as I go. Nudity doesn't bother either one of us. I've spent too much time in locker rooms with other swimmers to worry about somebody seeing what God gave me and Livvy doesn't have a modest bone in her body.

Truth be told, she's actually the only person besides the various doctors and my mother who has seen me completely naked since the bombing. My lower back is a mess of keloids from the injury and the many surgeries and I don't like people looking at them. It's one of the reasons why I stick to fast-hookups with guys and no sleepovers, my body gives away too many secrets. Invites too many unwanted questions.

"I'm at a six tonight." Zero is pain-free and I don't even remember what that feels like anymore. I walk into my bathroom and turn on the shower. "The episodes are increasing in frequency just like the doctor said they would."

The times when my mobility is limited is increasing, just as the doctors have all told me. I've seen them all, from every hospital in the U.S. and a few overseas and they all sing the final chorus in unison: the shrapnel will eventually cause paraplegia or kill me. They are all very sorry but there's nothing they can do for me.

There's one guy, a Dr. Bertrand from a hospital back east, who might be able to conduct an operation that can remove all the shrapnel from my body. I'd still have increasing mobility issues but the Grim Reaper would have to take a rain check. But the great Dr. B has looked at my records and turned me down for the surgery.

I step under the spray and Livvy comes in and sits down on the lid of the toilet to talk. We do this all the time and soon we won't be able to and the melancholy rains over my body with the water.

"I'm going to miss this when you move to NYC," I say, loud enough for her to hear me over the spray. "But I know Sarah is excited to finally have you with her."

"Two years apart was longer than we thought," she agrees, her tone chock full of the pain caused by living apart from your love. "I'm glad we made it. It was touch and go there for a while."

Sarah had moved to New York for her dream job in TV and Livvy still had two more years of school to finish and a scholarship she couldn't abandon. It had been tough on them and they'd had one six-week break-up that had been hard to watch.

"So, you didn't answer me," she changes the subject.

"Are the episodes worse?"

I pause, using the shield of the shower curtain to gather my thoughts. I know what she's asking me and I don't want to get into it tonight. It will kill my buzz before I even have one. I shut off the shower and pull back the fabric to grab a towel. I don't look at her.

"They are more frequent and it takes me longer to recover. The last one impacted my entire right leg and I couldn't walk for about an hour."

"Oh shit."

"Yep," I agree with her and move over to the mirror and wipe the condensation off with my towel. The face is still the same, the long hair a dark auburn because of the water weighing it down but I'm not the same. It's the eyes, the eyes give me away every time.

The medicine cabinet door squeaks a little when I swing it open to survey the contents inside. Deodorant, Neosporin, band aids, a tube of some eye cream I never use, sit alongside the double row of prescription pain killers, anti-inflammatories, and muscle relaxants. I use the toiletry items and shut the door, using the towel to get the excess water out of my hair.

"So, where do you want to go tonight?" Livvy's voice is behind me as I walk into my closet to find something to wear.

It's balls hot in Tennessee even when the sun goes down so I grab a white cotton sundress and pull it over my head. I wince a little bit at the pain that throbs in my right thigh because of the movement but I shake it off. My tits are small enough that I don't need a bra and I gave up underwear, unless I'm wearing formalwear or jeans, three years ago. Grabbing a pair of cowboy boots, I head back to the bathroom and find her gone. I swipe on my eyeliner, mascara and lip gloss and it's as good as it's gonna get tonight.

I head down the hall to Livvy's room and find her pulling up a pair of cutoff jean shorts. She has a t-shirt on that I gave her for Christmas which reads "Screw your 'lab safety'. I want superpowers". She'd rather kiss a man than put on makeup, so it looks like we're ready to go.

"I don't want to go to a club. Let's hit a party," I say as we both head into the living room of the apartment. We're three blocks off campus and it's the weekend between the two finals weeks. There's no need to go into Nashville proper if we want to party and I know where I want to go. "Let's go to Mateo and Zane's house."

Livvy stops rummaging through her small bag and looks up at me, the delight and surprise on her face emphasizing her doll-like resemblance.

"So, you're finally going to go to one of their parties? They've only invited you every time this entire year."

"Mateo never invited me, it's always Zane," I answer, transferring ID, lip gloss, breath mints, condoms, cash, and keys to my small party purse. I find what I'm really looking for in the side pocket, tucked into a semi-hidden space. I pull out the small manila envelope and peel back the flap, peering inside at the dozen small capsules nestled inside. I shake one out on my palm and pop it in my mouth, using a bottle of water to wash it down.

"What'd you take?" Livvy asks as she closes up her purse. She doesn't judge and she never nags but she does insist on knowing what I put in my system since she's my wingman. She also made me promise not to take anything stronger than smoking a joint without being with her. Since we're always together, that's not usually an issue.

"Molly." I don't drink alcohol, a holdover from my competitive training days and it's a bitch to have a hangover when I'm dealing with my other aches and pains. Harder drugs let me forget the pain for a while and I rarely have too much of an aftereffect.

She nods, not judging me, and waits while I put the last of my items in my party bag. Livvy doesn't always approve of how I live my life and she definitely isn't on board with my future plans but she supports me and stands by to make sure I don't go too far. I think it was all those years of pushing every limit life threw at me—body, mind, competitors—but

I'm wired to take it to the edge every single time. If it scares Livvy, she deserves an Oscar because I've never even seen a flicker of alarm in her brown eyes.

"So, any reason why you're throwing the 'boy wonders' a bone now?"

I don't know why she's playing coy. She knows why I've avoided going to Mateo Butler and Zane Wyatt's house all year. Hell, I've known it since the first time Mateo walked into my freshman Spanish class and announced he was the TA. Normally a girl who goes for long, lanky blondes, his six-feet two-inch, two hundred-pound, dark-haired package of lickable man would have knocked me on my ass if I hadn't already been sitting down. And then he locked his baby blues on mine and gave me his dimpled "I'm-going-to-fuck-you" smile and I knew I had to steer very clear of Mr. Butler.

T-R-O-U-B-L-E

From the jump, Mateo and I were the definition of chemistry. We'd circled each other for the entire year, through two semesters of Spanish and study groups. Because he intrigued me more than any other guy, I'd done my recon and watched him in class, around campus, and at the many clubs where Zane performed. At first glance, Mateo only took two things seriously: his beer, and his pussy.

But I watched him pretty closely and when he thought he wasn't on stage to perform for anybody, he was intense and pretty serious for a guy who didn't give a shit. I knew a faker when I saw one, I looked at one in the mirror every day.

I just shrug and answer, "Mateo Butler is nothing but trouble."

"Well, yeah, but that's usually the first required item on your list to give a guy the time of day."

"Oh no," I shake my head, slipping on my favorite pair of cowboys boots. Worn black leather with red flame accents on them, a gift from Aaron and the evidence of his love of my hair. "Mateo is the worst kind of trouble because under all that partying and screwing around is the worst kind of deception."

"I'm dying to hear this," Livvy says, not even trying to hide the sarcasm in her voice.

"Underneath all of it…" I pause for emphasis and while I'm camping it up, I couldn't be more serious, "…he's really a *nice* guy."

"Mother fucker," she says, her smile telling me that she gets me completely. "So, what are you going to do with this potential-boyfriend-material in manwhore's clothing?"

"I'm going to see if he's up for a little fun. No strings."

"And if he's not?"

I grab my purse and pull it across my body as I head to the door. "He's up for it."

Chapter Two

Mateo

"She's here."

I look up from my place on the couch in my room where I'm drinking a beer and considering the idea of letting Amy Tyne unzip my pants and blow me like she's been offering all night. I like Amy well enough and she gives great head even though she could watch the teeth more often, but I'm not into her tonight. We started out two years ago as casual fuck buddies at my fraternity house. If I wasn't hooking up with someone else and she wasn't with somebody, we'd meet up and exchange orgasms for an hour or three. She'd come and leave and not call. It was awesome.

About six months ago we hooked up in an alley outside a downtown club and ever since then she's been texting, calling, showing up at my house "just to hang out". Tonight she invited me to a graduation brunch with her family and every single alarm I have went off in my head.

"Who's here?" I ask, pushing Amy off my lap and placing my empty beer bottle on my beat up coffee table. I stand, hoping he means who I think he means.

"Ariel." Zane waggles his eyebrows and uses the nickname we have for the woman who has been on my radar since she stepped into freshman Spanish. He's the one who started calling her Ariel and I have to admit the stupid joke makes sense. She has red hair, emerald green eyes and was a world-class swimmer until a bunch of assholes with a bomb decided to blow the athlete's village to kingdom come. "She's here with her roommate."

"It only took her all year," I say, moving past my best friend to go find the object of my lust and late night fantasies and see if she is ready to act some of them out with me.

"What about me?" Amy says from my couch, her words slurring a bit with the beer she's been drinking all night. "What about brunch?"

"I don't like brunch. Sorry." I walk out, closing the door behind me.

"You love brunch," Zane says as we head down the stairs to the party on the first floor.

"Yeah, but I hate parents."

"Only because they all love you."

It's true. I think it's the manners my folks drilled into me since I was a kid that makes all the mama's picture me as the perfect guy for their daughter. Not me. I'm not the guy you should rely on to be there through the "for better or for worse" part of anything.

Our house is always full of people but tonight is nuts because everyone is celebrating the end of the school year. Another week of exams, then graduation and college life will be over and I'll have to join the ranks of those who pretend to be adults while figuring their shit out. I might be in medical school. I might not. I'm enrolled but I just can't visualize walking into the building and actually doing it. That was the plan before my sister died but now... it doesn't feel like my thing anymore. The whole thing stresses me out so I push it out of the way and scan the crowd for Carlisle Queen.

She's easy to spot. Tall, long-legged but it's her hair that grabs my attention. Not just red, it's at least four shades of auburn and shot through with gold. I want to grab it, wrap it around my fingers. A couple of times a curl brushed against my arm in study group and my dick got hard like I was some kid in high school. I'm not ashamed to admit it; this girl does it for me. Period.

"Whoa buddy. Aren't you even going to try and play it cool?" Zane asks, right on my heels.

I follow her progress through the house, hanging back when she stops in the kitchen, waiting as her best friend grabs a red solo cup and gets in line for the keg. She makes no move to get one for herself and I'm not surprised. Carlisle doesn't drink and the rumor is that she prefers recreational drugs when she parties. I think she's come to class stoned a couple of times but I can't prove it.

"I don't think the Ice Queen likes head games," I say using the nickname she earned from the student body within the first few weeks of fall semester after she quickly shut down all invitations from the sororities and refused every date offer she received. I've watched it all from a distance and learned from their mistakes. Just like the one my buddy Pete and his roommate Seth are making right now.

"Hey. You're Carlisle Queen, right?" Pete asks continuing with the introductions after she nods. "This is Seth."

"Hi," she says, making the briefest eye contact before she scans the room. In anticipation of our eyes meeting, my skin prickles with the low burn of awareness that always happens when I'm within five feet of her.

When her gaze slides to mine the surge of adrenaline burns off every bit of the beer buzz I am feeling. When a slight smile tilts up her full lips I get the signal she's sending loud and clear: she's here for me and the game we've been playing is finally on. My dick is hard as a spike but the knowledge of how this night is going to end calms me and I lean against the door frame to watch what happens.

"This is Olivia," Carlisle introduces her roommate to the guys when the other woman appears at her side with her beer.

The guys nod at the newcomer but Pete is all about Carlisle and he steps into her personal space. She looks like she might retreat but instead she extends her hand out and lightly pushes him back the step he just took and one more for good measure. I laugh and nod when Zane murmurs "taking him out like a boss" in my ear.

"We were thinking of going back to our place and partying some more. You want to go?" Pete asks, his words slurring a little. He was one of the first to arrive tonight and he's hammered back at least a beer every half-hour. I'll probably find him passed out in my bathtub in the morning.

"We hear you like to party."

He means that he's heard she likes to party and fuck. Carlisle has a good time. Never with college guys. Locals and musicians only.

"You're friend can come too," Seth says, nodding towards Olivia. "The bed's big enough for four."

I give him guts for just throwing that out there but if Carlisle looked any less interested, she'd be catatonic.

"Sorry. I don't like penis," Olivia answers, taking a long sip from her beer while throwing an "are you kidding me" look at Carlisle.

Carlisle chuckles and shakes her head. "No thanks guys. I've already got my fun lined up for the night."

She flicks a glance in my direction and I know she's talking about me. My whole body relaxes and tenses up with desire all the same time. I move forward to rescue her from the "B-team" when Pete steps in it with his two big feet.

"Can I see your medals? Are they at your place?"

"Oh no," Zane mumbles beside me and we both shake or heads.

It's commonly known that Carlisle doesn't like talking about the games, her medals, or anything about that part of her life. She wants to put all that behind her and I don't blame her. Everything she accomplished is overshadowed by what happened in the end. She just wants to forget.

And the look she's giving Seth right now says that I need to intervene before she gets his blood all over my kitchen floor.

I step forward and insert myself in between them. I look down at her but I speak directly to him.

"Hey Seth, move on buddy."

"Mateo man, stop cock blocking me."

I smile at Carlisle and she smiles back, the flash of her emerald eyes wicked and I know tonight is going to be fun. As soon as I get rid of Seth.

"Seth, she's here to see me so you need to go and stop cock blocking *me*."

He mutters some random curses but leaves anyway. He grabs another beer that he doesn't need before he and his flunkie walk off in a huff.

"If you were at all intrigued by the threesome, I think I can accommodate you," I lean down and murmur in her ear.

"Maybe another night." She reaches up and grabs the lapel of my shirt and drags me closer, whispering fiercely in my ear. "I think you'll be more than enough tonight, yes?"

"Fuck yeah I will." I reach down and wrap my arm around her waist, keeping her close to me. She is warm, smells like gardenias, and her breast is heavy against my side. I have no interest in delaying this one minute longer. "Come with me."

I take her out onto the deck. There are fewer people here and I find a quiet corner where I can touch her and talk to her without interruption.

"You want anything to drink?"

"Nope." She places her water bottle on the railing. "That's not my preferred buzz."

"I've heard that."

"You've been checking up on me."

"I hear things." I smile and lean down until our forehead touch heads and I can feel her breath on my face. She steps into me and I place my hands on her hips. We fit together perfectly and I can't help but imagine how good it will be when all these clothes are out of the way. "I thought you wouldn't be here tonight because *you* have a Spanish exam on Monday."

I want to kiss the corner of her mouth where her lips form a tease of a smile. "I'm going to ace the written exam." Her smile droops a little. "The verbal portion... it might get ugly."

That is an understatement. I have never heard anyone butcher the Spanish language like Carlisle Queen. Yes, I'm biased because I grew up in a bilingual household but she is terrible. I once thought you'd have to work hard to pronounce things as badly as she does. Not Carlisle. For her, it comes naturally.

I open up a little space in between us but I keep my hands on her hips, even letting the right one dip to cup the sexy, round swell of her ass.

"I think you need to practice. Use me." When one auburn eyebrow lifts I smile at her dirty mind. "That's for later. Show me what you've got."

"*Me gustaría pedir del menu,*" she says and I strain a muscle hiding my wince.

"Okay, so you want to order from a menu." I nod and when her eyes light up with hope, I shake it in the negative. "That was awful. Try again." I demonstrate the proper way to say it and then urge her to try again. "Don't pick some random sentence. Just talk to me. Tell me what you want me to know."

She considers me for a moment and then the wicked gleam is back and she steps even closer to me. "*Creo que eres caliente*".

She thinks I'm hot. Good to know.

"Better," I murmur. "Try another."

"*Quiero saber cómo te gusto.*"

She wants to know how I taste.

I groan as she leans in close, her lips hovering over mine a demonstration of what she wants. I want it too. I chase her mouth but she partially turns her face to the side while keeping her eyes locked on mine. Her hands are on my chest and I know she can feel the pounding in my chest at her next practice line.

"Te quiero a ti dentro de mí."

Fuck. She wants me inside her.

"That's what I want too. To be inside you, to feel your long legs wrapped around my waist." I trace her lips with my tongue, capturing her own moan on the tip and savoring her surrender. "Come with me. I want to touch you and I'm not doing it with an audience."

I enter the door we just passed through and lead her down the back hallway, heading for the stairs and my bedroom. I make it halfway down the deserted hallway and I can't wait another minute. I push her against the wall, raising one arm to bracket us in. She tips her head to look up at me and I get lost for a moment in her eyes. Usually the color of emerald, they are nearly black with her arousal. Her gaze flickers down to my mouth and I grin.

"*Voy a besarte ahora*," I whisper, the only warning of what I'm about to do. She understands me, her breath catching just before I angle my head and take her mouth.

The kiss is hard, bruising, devouring. Months of pent-up desire and want vented in the press of mouths, the lashing of wet tongues, the clink of teeth. She moans under me and clutches the fabric of my t-shirt, pulling me closer as I dive in deeper, dominating her with my craving invasion.

She pulls back to breath, her breasts rising and falling against my chest as she struggles to catch her breath. Her lips are already a deep rose and I want nothing more than to see them wrapped around my cock.

"*Quiero más.* She wants more and she just takes it.

I groan as one of her hands travels up my body and around my neck to pull me down to her. Her lips slant over mine and I slide my tongue into her wet heat. This time it is slower, softer but the gradual build of possession flips my switch and I slide my hands over her ass and angle her pelvis forward, grinding my erection against her sex.

It is intoxicating. The curves of her body inviting me to explore with my hands. I trace the sides of her torso, ending only when I can cup her breasts in my palms, thumbs rubbing the hard nipples pressing against the thin cotton of her dress.

Carlisle breaks off the kiss, throwing her head back to bare her neck to me and I press my lips to her throat. I drop my right hand back to her ass, under her dress where I find bare flesh and nothing else.

"Fuck Carlisle," I slip my hand a little lower, into the hot cleft of her body. "You're pussy is so wet for me." I groan when she opens her legs wider and presses her ass back on my roving hand. "I want in there so bad."

"Where's your room?" She pants against my mouth, her

tongue slipping in for a quick taste before retreating to let me answer.

"Upstairs."

"Too fucking far." She breaks off the kiss and looks over my shoulder, her eyes zeroing in on the empty laundry behind us. "In there."

She doesn't have to ask me twice and I spin us both, covering the three steps necessary to reach in the room and shut the door behind us. I shove her back against it and fumble for the lock in the dark, finally succeeding in sliding it home.

I find her mouth in the dark and lift her up my body, encouraging her to wrap her legs around my waist. She whimpers and I shudder in response to the carnal sound as I begin a slow thrust against her exposed sex. I lose myself in the kiss, her taste, the grind of our bodies together. When she wedges her hand between us and strokes my cock through my jeans, I lower her to the ground and release her from the kiss.

Eyes adjusted to the dark I can see her eyes, glassy with her desire and they way she never loses eye contact when her hands undo the button and ease the zipper down. Her fingers wrap around my aching cock and I shudder with the exquisite pleasure/pain of her touch.

"Fuck Carlisle. You get me so hard."

"You're so big," she murmurs, her voice a deeper, huskier version of her usual tone. I like the way she says my name. "Mateo, I want this in my mouth. Can I?"

"Oh my God, yes. Please."

I stare as my dream girl drops to her knees in front of me and drags my jeans down to the middle of my thighs. She leans forward and licks a long, wet line from the root to the crown and across the slit.

I fumble beside me for the light switch and I flip it up. The light bulbs are cheap so the light is watery and shadowy but it does the job. I can see everything.

"I want to watch you suck me off," I say, inhaling sharply when she leans back in and takes my erection deep into her mouth. Lips clamped tight around my flesh she bobs her head up and down, the rhythm slow but leading to that slow burn in my balls, in my belly. Her fingers dig into my ass cheeks, the light tug encouraging me to thrust into her wet heat. I raise my hands, my fingers sliding into the silky, red-gold strands as I watched her take all of me.

Fuck, you're beautiful," I gasp, overcome by lust when her eyes meet mine from across the distance of my body. I know this image will be branded on my brain until the day I die. "So fucking gorgeous."

The burn in my belly intensifies and I realize I don't want to come this way. I pull out of her mouth and lift her to her feet, kissing her and moaning at the taste of me in her mouth.

"I need to be inside you. I need to know if you feel as good as the dreams that leave me hard and aching. I want to see if you're as good as the fantasies I have running through my head as I come all over myself."

She leans up and kisses me hard and fierce, pulling back to hand over a condom and a promise. "I'm better. I guarantee it."

***

Carlisle

I thought we'd be this hot together and I wasn't wrong.

I'm a shivering, aroused mess and watching Mateo roll on the condom is just about the sexiest thing I've ever seen. He's long and thick and I can still taste him on my tongue.

"I want you so much," Mateo huffs out on a breath before he takes my lips again in a kiss. His fingers, rough against the skin of my thighs lift my skirt as he backs me up until I am leaning against the washing machine. He strokes upward, his touch causing goosebumps all over my skin. There is no hesitation as he finds my folds and caresses my flesh. I arch into his hand, encouraging the digit he eases inside me on a slow pump. "You're soaking wet for me. I love that."

He leans over me, his mouth devouring the skin where my neck meets my shoulder. Soft nips and harder bites leaves me writhing on the hand still buried between my legs. It is so good and I can feel the blaze and tingle of a fantastic orgasm building with every thrust of the two fingers he's using to fuck me. He is hitting all the best spots, the slow guide he's using is designed to torture me if his grin is any indication.

"Teo, keep doing that. Please," I beg. I want what he's dying to give me and I'm not ashamed to ask for it.

His kisses travel lower on my body, his free hand pulling aside the top of my dress and exposing my swollen breasts to his attention. His lips closed around my right nipple and I come, hard and long, surprising us both. He groans but keeps tugging on it with his teeth extending the waves of pleasure through several amazing aftershocks.

"Look at me Carlisle," he demands, his voice sexy with his want. I lift my eyes to his and I'm lost in the dark navy they have transformed into with what I've done to him. "That was gorgeous. You are amazing when you come and I could watch you all night long."

He lifts me top of the washer and steps in between my legs, his erection pressed against the place where I want him the most. He leans forward and kisses me, soft and tender as he enters my body in one slow push. We exhale together, our breaths meshing with the slide of our tongues against each other. I loop my hands around his neck, weaving my fingers in his hair as I pull him deeper inside me.

The stretch at his invasion reminds me of why I love sex. The pleasure, the slow burn building into a molten heat that runs throughout my entire body. Fucking heaven on earth.

"Make me come again, Teo. Please."

He groans and his thrusts become harder, more forceful. I'm making lots of noise, unable to contain the moans and pants he drives out of me with every thrust of his hips. I can't help it. He is *that* good. It's a good thing that the party is so loud.

"Fuck Carlisle, you're so fucking tight." He loses his grip on me and overcorrects, jamming me against the washing machine, causing it to slide backwards and hit the wall with a loud thud. We both laugh as he keeps thrusting, enjoying the hell out of each other as he starts to come. "Oh my God."

His hands grab my ass cheeks and lift me higher against him, the angle now the perfect position for his rock hard body to rub against my clit and I'm so primed that I join him in the freefall. His mouth on my nipple, the hard suckling sends delicious aftershock shivers throughout my body and I arch into it, my hands twisting in his hair to keep him there as long as possible.

His thrusts slow down, evolving into shallow dips and swivel of his hips against mine. I grind back, enjoying the pleasure still sparking with each rub against my clit. I slide my hands down to his ass and squeeze, relishing the way the muscles become concave with every forward push.

"Sweet holy hell," I breathe out, my heart racing in my chest like a freight train. "I don't know if it's you or the Molly but I am tingling all over. Damn."

He releases my nipple, lifts his head, and grins down at me. "It's me, of course."

"Absolutely," I nod and pull him to me to for a long slow kiss of tongues and teeth and more laughter. "I don't think I've ever come while laughing before."

"Imagine what we can do if we make it to a bed," he murmurs in my ear. "Your place or mine?" When I don't answer right away he pulls back to look at my face. "What?"

This is where it gets awkward.

"Usually I'm a one and done girl."

His hand strokes lightly across my collarbone and dips down to circle and gently squeeze my nipple. I gasp and he takes another kiss. "No exceptions? I think I'm worth an exception." He adds a sexy, teasing growl to his plea. "I haven't a chance to taste your pussy. You can't go until I show you my mad oral skills. You won't regret it."

I slump against him with desire and try to hide my smile and hang on to my principles while he touches me. I want to stay, want to invite him back to my bed but I have my rules for a reason. For his protection more than mine.

I shove back and shake my head, adjusting my top to cover my breasts and give me some breathing space to make the hard call.

"I don't stay over. I don't do beds. I don't date," I shrug at his raised eyebrow, smiling to ease the sting. "Those are my rules."

Mateo watches as I ease out of his arms, adjusting my dress. I'm having trouble meeting his gaze, afraid that he'll see the desire to make an exception on my face. This is why I waited until he was almost gone; I knew I'd want to break my rules for Mateo. I have a crush. There is no point in denying it. But it is also the main reason I need to leave.

"Well, when you put it that way, you're almost challenging me to get you to break them," He says, leaning against the washer with his arms crossed over his broad chest.

His dark hair is mussed, his jeans pulled up but unfastened so I can still see the top of his cock and the dark curls at its base. My mouth actually waters and I hesitate, regreatting that I'd waited all year to sample his goodies and now I was just walking away.

I lean down and grab the purse that fell to the ground when we burst into the room.

"Sorry, I'm very firm on 'no beds, no sleepovers, no dates' rule.

"I should warn you that I am a very creative guy when I want to be." He grins even wider and I realize that I might have bitten off more than I can chew with him. "I'm also very creative."

"*Darle su mejor tiro mateo,*" I say, daring him to give it his best effort.

And then I leave, wondering what I've gotten myself into with Mateo Butler.

Chapter Three

Carlisle

Going to see Dr. Shrieve once a month is a compromise with my parents.

I left Texas and came to Nashville to go to college because I couldn't stay with April and John Queen one minute longer without committing a crime that would have gotten me the death penalty in the Lone Star state. They are good people, the best parents, but they were smothering me.

I can only imagine how terrifying it must have been for them to see me hurt in the bombing. I remember times in the hospital when I woke in the middle of the night to find my mother crying in the chair next to my bed.

So I cannot blame them for being protective.

But after the initial shock, the agony of the surgeries and physical therapy, they refused to make the turn and see me as a grown woman. They hovered, they worried, they were on my ass like a tailgater on the freeway and I couldn't take it anymore.

I applied to and enrolled in Nashville University against their protest but agreed to continue to see a therapist to deal with my PTSD and other issues.

It was an easy compromise to get away and live my life on my own terms.

Dr. Shrieve is in her mid-thirties, married with no children but two very spoiled Chesapeake Bay Retrievers. She is plain-speaking and encourages me to be the same. I like her. If she wasn't my doctor, we'd be friends.

"So, are you dating?" she asks, looking down at her notebook with a slight smile tugging at her lips. She asks me this every time. The answer is always the same.

"I don't date. You know this," I answer as I snag another Twizzler from the pack on the table. "I did it with the TA in my Spanish class. In his laundry room. It was awesome."

She raises her eyebrows, smiling as she looks at me over the edge of the notebook. "I thought you weren't going to do that."

"I wasn't but it's the end of the school year and he's graduating."

"So, he's another emotionally and logistically unavailable man you allow yourself to be with in an environment that you control from initiation to completion."

"Wow. Are you charging by the big word today?" I shift on the couch, adjusting my position until the low throb in my back reduces from "give me a Percocet" to "give me a stiff shot of whiskey". "We've talked about this. I love sex. I want to have an active sex life but I don't want to get involved with anyone. I can't."

"I just think you might be passing on the opportunity to have a real connection with someone. True intimacy is not found in the alley behind a bar or in a guy's laundry room. Don't you want that kind of connection?"

"I've had that, Doc. I had it and I watched him die right in front of me with his blood and brains all over my hands." I swallow hard, the memories I rarely indulge in making it difficult to speak. "I'm not doing that again."

"You're not even allowing yourself the chance to do it again." She's stubborn this one. Determined for me to get that happily-ever-after she lives in the suburbs. "You've mentioned this TA so many times over the past year. I just wonder if there is something there to pursue."

I take a bite of the candy and consider Mateo. He's hot, intense, a smartass. If I was the old Carlisle, he'd be a guy I'd want in my bed, on dates, taking home to meet April and John. The new Carlisle needs to keep it all physical and as far away from entanglement as possible. I have nothing else to offer. "It's not a good idea. It's not fair to do that to somebody."

"So, you're still planning on taking your own life." It isn't really a question. I worried at first that she'd tell my parents or try to get me locked up but she explained that there's a difference between suicidal ideation due to mental illness and planned suicide. She's not on board with assisted suicide for herself but her east-coast-educated-yuppie upbringing won't allow her to trample on my right to choose.

We've been over and over this countless times and I throw my hands up in the air in a "really" gesture.

"Look, I wouldn't be much of a shrink if I didn't ask you about it at least every other session." She reaches over and steals a candy from my bag. "I know you're not crazy and you're not depressed. But there aren't many young women your age who plan to end their life."

"The doctors all say that I have a forty percent chance of the shrapnel doing it for me. If that is how I go, my pill stash will go to waste. I'll leave it to you in my will if you want."

"You're avoiding my point about the other sixty percent."

"I don't want to be in a wheelchair for the rest of my life." I start out looking her in the eye and then I can't anymore. She tries to hide it but I can see the pity in her gaze. It's the same look I get from every reporter, every doctor, every person I've met since the bombing. "I just don't want to live that way."

"Lots of people live with disabilities."

"And they are much better people than I am." I can't control the anger in my voice. I am really tired of explaining this again.

"I'm not saying you're a bad person. I just feel like I should continue to make sure you're aware of the options for you. Paralysis is not the end of your life. You can even participate in competitive athletics again. The Paralympics—"

I stand, biting back the wince in my right leg as I gather up my things. "I've told you at least eight million fucking times. All of that... swimming... it's behind me. You say I'm not crazy and it's because I left my past in the past and I made peace about my future. I live in the here and now more than most people, milking enjoyment out of every fucking minute."

"I didn't mean to make you angry," she says, putting her pen and notebook down on the table in front of her. "You're so young and you've got your whole life ahead of you."

"And you need to accept the fact that my 'whole life' is just going to be a lot shorter than expected." I look at her and hope she'll hear me. "I have and I'm okay with it. Really."

She stares me down and I can see the wheels in her head spinning in every possible direction. I know she doesn't really understand. How could she? Nobody can unless they've lived it and I sincerely hope that no one ever has to go through what I did. Never again.

But those assholes took more than my health, more than my career and passion, more than the man I loved. They took my control, took away my ability to form my own future. They took away my hope that each day can get better... because mine has never gotten better. It's lke I'm stuck in that moment when I knew Aaron was gone and I was left behind to bear the pain of our loss all by myself.

The timer goes off on her phone, signaling the end of our session and I let out a sigh of relief. I bend over to get my purse off the floor and I gasp at the sharp pain in my leg. I test out the sensation, tapping my foot on the floor and measuring my level of control. It hurts but I don't feel the tingle of numbness in my leg that signals another episode of limited mobility.

"You okay?" Dr. Shrieve asks, reaching out a hand that she quickly pulls back. She knows I'll ask for help if I need it.

"Nothing a little smoke break with MaryJane won't cure," I joke, biting back a laugh when her eyebrows shoot up at the mention of my recreational drug habit. She's lectured me about it before, many times, and I can't resist the chance to yank her chain.

"You didn't smoke before you came here? I'm honored." The level of sarcasm dripping from every word is epic.

"What? How helpful would it be for me to come to my therapy session high as a kite?" I tease, both of us recalling the time I showed up loaded on a dose of Molly. The good doctor was not amused and sent me home in a cab and a bill for the full session.

"I'll see you in a month," she says and points at the door. She tries to remain stern but I see her smile as I open the door that leads directly into the hallway of the office building and bypasses the waiting area of her office. It'd a privacy thing. Nobody wants to parade their crazy in front of a bunch of strangers.

I walk to the elevator and press the button for lobby, leaning on the wall a little bit as my back twinges. Once I get to campus, I'll find Livvy, go home and light up my little stash OG Kush marijuana I bought from a contact in California. It was helpful with the pain and the anxiety I experienced when my legs stopped working, however temporary.

I love this city and a few minutes later I am enjoying the ride as the bus takes me through downtown Nashville, stopping often to discharge or accept new passengers. I peer out of the window, soaking up the sights as we pass Music Row. Numerous musicians walk down the sidewalk, guitar cases slung over their shoulders. I wonder if they have melodies and words swirling around in their heads as they make their way home or to work or the next gig. Can they turn it off or does it keep them up at night until they get it all down on paper? I am a music junkie and those kinds of questions fascinate me. It was one of the reasons I chose to move to Nashville.

Swimming was like that for me. As I got closer to competition, I would plan the race in my head, committing the strategy and the strengths and weaknesses of my opponents in the database in my brain. I would practice the strokes in and out of the pool, committing the movement to muscle memory. The constant soundtrack in *my* head was the sound of the water rushing past my ears and my elevated, ecstatic heartbeat.

I miss that music. I miss the cool water on my skin, the weightless power of my body in it, the strength I exerted as I carved my path through it. I never really heard the crowds yelling or my coach screaming. Just the damn water music, my theme song.

It's why I've never been in a pool since the attack. I haven't heard the music since that day. The moment when the bomb went off it turned my paradise into a nightmare.

The bus rumbles to a stop on campus near the science building where Livvy is taking her final exam and I exit, steadying myself against the doorframe when my right foot hits the sidewalk and I lose balance.

"You okay, miss?" the driver asks, the beads on the end of her cornrow braids clinking together as she gets up to lend me a hand. Her touch is light, tentative and I give her a smile as I push away and stand on my own.

"I'm fine. A touch of vertigo," I answer as she returns to her seat. "Thanks."

I walk as far as I can, each step increasing the lack of sensation and control over my leg. My heart is hammering in my chest, sweat forming on my back and under my arms as I fight off the panic attack I can feel building in my gut. I don't know what's worse, the actual loss of mobility or the fear that this might be the time it doesn't come back.

I make it to the common area outside of Livvy's building and grab onto the back of a bench, lurching around it until I'm in position to sit down. I'm winded and my hands are shaking as I rub over my leg, cursing the pins and needles crawling over my skin. I flex my right leg, relieved to see that it obeys my command and lifts a few inches off the ground. The pain when I do this is sharp but I don't care about it.

It's the lack of feeling, pain or otherwise, that I fear. The pain is a old friend.

I pull my phone out of my purse and check the time.

Another hour until Livvy is done and there is no way I can pull her out of a final. I'll sit here and wait, grateful that the weather is fine and the sun is warm on my shoulders. I shift on the hard bench, adjusting my position to ease the pain in my back, gasping when it jabs me deep. I almost double over with it, my hand in a white knuckle grip on the arm of the bench.

"Carlisle?"

A large body blocks the sun and I shiver with the loss of warmth and the aftershock as the wave of pain subsides. I gulp in air, slowing down my pants as I fight to gain control of the pain like they taught me in pain management class. I open my eyes, noting the sticky wetness of tears on my lashes, and find Mateo looking down at me.

His expression immediately morphs into concern and he drops to one knee beside me. He reaches out and touches my hand and I grab it, holding on as if he can keep the ground under my feet.

"What do you need?" he asks and I almost cry at the relief I feel knowing he is here.

"My leg." I motion to the traitorous limb and wince as another wave of pain hits me. "It hurts. I need to get home but I can't walk."

"Do you need an ambulance?"

"No."

He stares at me for a few seconds before squeezing my hand. "Can you wait here while I get my car? I'll take you home."

"I can wait."

"I'll be right back." He leans in and brushes a soft kiss against my forehead before he goes and I whimper at the loss of the comfort his presence brought me for those few seconds. I sit on the bench, practicing my yoga breathing and cursing the fact I usually skipped yoga in favor of watching *Saved by the Bell* episodes with Livvy. Fuck you Zack Morris.

A blue car pulls up to the curb and Mateo hops out, slamming his door and then running over to me.

"How do you want to do this? I can carry you but I don't want to hurt you." I look up at him, horrified by the suggestion and it must be so apparent that he chuckles a little. "Okay, I won't carry you." He kneels down by me once again. "You're tall so you might be able to link your arm around my neck and I can support you that way. It will look like I'm copping a feel but I think my reputation can take the hit."

Even through the pain, he makes me smile and I nod at his suggestion. "Let's try that."

Mateo grabs my right arm and loops it over his shoulders, his left arm tight around my waist and we slowly rise to a standing position. With him supporting me, I don't have to put any pressure on my right leg and the pain subsides a little.

"Is this okay?"

"Yeah, thank you."

"I would say my pleasure but it will be all yours in a few seconds." We make slow progress across the quad and he nods towards his car. "That's a fully restored 1964 Chevy Impala with a convertible top and I feel like I should warn you that you might have the urge to fall in love with me once you ride in her."

I laugh, rolling my eyes at his ridiculous banter. "I think I can resist."

"I wouldn't rush to judgment." He leans over and opens the passenger door, hooking my legs behind the knees and lowering me into the seat with the grace of a groom carrying his bride over the threshold. I flail a little at being man-handled but he looks at me and shrugs. "It sits low to the ground and I figured it would put too much strain on your leg to get in the regular way."

He shuts my door before I can reply and sprints around to his side and slides behind the wheel. I buckle my seatbelt as he starts up the engine and I can't help the "ohhh" that escapes my mouth when the huge engine purrs and vibrates the entire car like one of those massage chairs at the mall. The leather is supple and hugs every part of me and the chrome shines so much I can see my reflection in it.

"I love this car," I say as he pulls out into traffic. His driving is so smooth and the car rides like a boat, not one jolt causes me extra pain.

He glances over at me and grins. "I told you."

"I said I was in love with the car, not you."

"It's only a matter of time." He grins and pulls the car over and to a stop. I look out the window and realize we are at my apartment. I look back at him and he grins. "The ride was free but the distraction from the pain will cost you."

I snicker as he gets out of the car and heads over to my side. I undo my seatbelt and open my door but he stops me before I can get out.

"Are you up to it?"

"I'm not sure."

"Then that is a no. You want to do it the same as before but in reverse?" he asks, kneeling down to get to the right level. "Let's try it."

I loop my arms around his neck and he puts an arm under both of my knees and gently wedges the other behind my back. He lifts and a lightning strike of pain runs down my leg and I gasp. He stops immediately, his lips against the skin of my temple as he murmurs soothing noises and apologies.

"Jesus. I'm sorry." He adjusts his position around me, his dark head bent and his nose gliding softly against my jaw. I remember he did the same thing after we had sex. A sweet touch after all the sizzling heat. I want to burrow deeper into his embrace, lean on his strength for a little while longer.

Which means I need to get away from him as soon as possible. I have no business starting anything with this nice guy in party boy clothing. If I keep this up, I might want to keep him.

"I think I'm good," I say and when he looks at me, I nod to give him the go-ahead. "I'm on the second floor. There's an elevator."

"You got it." He lifts me slowly, watching my face closely to gauge my pain level. Once he is fully upright he kicks the door shut with his foot and starts the short trip to my place. There's no one around so the elevator comes quickly and with just a few moments of wincing pain, we are at my door and he's unlocking it and carrying me inside.

"Where do you want to be? Couch?"

"Yep." I wave at the longer chaise end of our sectional. "Over there. I can put my feet up."

He lowers me to the couch and we both sigh with relief. I lie back on the cushions and close my eyes. Thank God I'm home.

"Mateo, can you get my meds?" I ask, popping one eye open to find him looking down at me with a worried expression on his face. "What?"

"Are you sure you don't want to go to the doctor?"

"No. I'm used to this now. It's a result of my injury and all the surgeries. I'll be fine in a little while."

He stares at me for a minute, probably deciding whether he believes me or not. Decision made he claps his hands together. "Okay where are your meds?"

"First room on the right. Right hand side table, top drawer."

He heads off in the direction of my bedroom and I hear the slide of the drawer as it opens. A pause and then the question I know is coming.

"Carlisle, there's only a few baggies of pot in here."

"There's one with a couple of rolled joints. That's the one I need."

I hear the drawer slide shut and his footsteps as he returns to me, my bag of joints in his hand.

"You don't have a prescription you can take?" he asks, handing over the bag when I waggle my fingers at him.

"I do but they knock me out. I don't want to sleep, I just want the pain to go away." I fish a lighter out of the purse lying beside me and light up, patiently coaxing the smoke that will make the bad man go away. I get it going and inhale deeply, holding it in until I have to breathe. I offer it to Mateo. "You want some?"

"Not my thing but thanks." He pauses, looking around my living room and I expect his next comment to be "nice place" or something like that but it isn't. "You get high a lot, yeah?"

"I wouldn't say a lot but probably more than the average. The pot helps me with the pain and the other... " I shrug. "... I just like it."

I take another drag and wait him out. He's got something he wants to ask and I'd bet my favorite pair of Chuck's that it's going to be about my medals.

"Is the pain bad?"

I am wrong. Color me surprised. Pleasantly.

"I have a low throb or aches all the time. The scar tissue from the surgeries are the worst but the nerve pain is the one that fucking brings me to my knees."

"That sucks."

"It really does." I settle back against the cushions and close my eyes, starting to feel the effects of the drug on my system. "I do not recommend getting blown up."

"I'll keep that in mind." Laughing, he walks over to me and presses another one of those damn soft kisses to my forehead. I keep my eyes shut and I am all about the other senses.

He smells awesome, a combination of cologne and something delicious, and I lean into it. I remember every kiss, every touch, every thrust of that night and with the MaryJane relaxing me, my body is responding in all the best ways to his proximity. He pulls away and I almost whimper at the loss of sensation but it's for the best. I can't get involved with anyone, it's my number one rule.

"Well, I've got to go out to my cousin's house and help him with some drywall. You gonna be okay?" he asks.

I open my eyes, blinking up at him in the bright sunlight spilling into the room. I'm starting to feel good with the pain subsiding to low throb. "I'm good. Thanks so much for helping me out."

"You're welcome." He hesitates and then reaches down

and grabs my phone off the couch beside me. He thumbs it on and starts typing.

I laugh and reach for my phone; he zigs when I zag and I can't get it. "What are you doing?"

"I'm programming my number in your phone. Call me if you need anything. I'm your backup wingman when Livvy isn't around." He hands my phone back to me with a sexy grin and wink of those fucking gorgeous baby blues.

If I could get my hands on him right now, I'd bite and lick him all over. So, it's probably a good thing that I can't off this couch.

"Hey, thanks. Again."

He starts backing up to the door. "Call me. We can grab something to eat."

I shake my head, unable to stop smiling. I blame it entirely on the pot. "That sounds too much like a date."

"Labels. You are so hung up on labels." He smiles and steps through the door. "Call me."

"I won't."

But I'm starting to wish I could.

Chapter Four

Mateo

"Hey Mateo, did you get a contact high or something?" Max asks.

I jolt out of my thoughts to find my cousin and Zane staring at me from across the bedroom where we are hanging and taping drywall. This old farmhouse belonged to my grandparents before my grandma died and Max bought it from him. He lives here with his fiancée, Kit Landry, a bona fide country music star who fights for the top spots with Taylor and Miranda. They are planning to have their wedding in this house, so I've been recruited to help out. He pays in beer and pizza and front row seats at her shows, so it's a pretty even trade.

But today I'm not pulling my weight. I am cold busted. I drifted off, completely immersed in the constant replay of what happened today with Carlisle.

"Sorry, I just keep thinking about today." I place the taping knife in the mud pan and place it on the makeshift table holding the bulk of our materials and wipe my hands on my jeans. I grab a Gatorade from the cooler and toss one to each them. I told them about what happened the minute I arrived. "She's just... "

I don't know how to describe Carlisle Queen. The woman was on the Wheaties box so we all think we know her. And she was the center of the coverage that followed the bombing. She wasn't the only athlete who survived the bombing but her story was always the lead. A few hours after she stepped off the podium with her twelfth gold medal, she was in a hospital in Germany fighting for her life and grieving the loss of her friends and lover.

Aaron Daniels and Carlisle were America's sweethearts. Two kids who'd trained together for years at the same facility in Baltimore, they'd fallen in love in the public eye and everyone ate it up. I wasn't the only guy who thought Aaron was the luckiest fucker in the world. And now I had a small idea of just lucky he'd been and I wanted more than just one taste.

I sigh. "She's got me by the fucking balls, Max."

"The sex was *that* good?" He asks, lowering his bulky frame down to the floor. He's a big guy, we grow them big in the Butler family and his size helps with his job as a firefighter. We grew up together and he knows me as well as Zane does. "I know how much sex you've had, so I'm throwing the bullshit flag."

"He's blinded by the glitter of 'new pussy'," Zane adds from his perch on top of a big container or paint. "Blown out of normal proportions by the fact that he's had a crush on her since the nanosecond she walked into his class. It's kinda cute."

I flip them both the bird because nothing expresses my reaction to their comments any better than that. The fact that they aren't entirely wrong keeps me from hauling them outside into the yard and kicking their asses.

"Yes, the sex *was* that good but she's fun. Smart. She keeps me at arm's length, even when I'm helping her. There's this wall up. You can see through it and you can even touch her but it keeps you from getting too close." I have no idea if that makes any sense to them but it does to me.

"So, it's the thrill of the chase," Zane comments, nodding his head in understanding. "I get why she keeps reeling you in. It's not like you to go back for seconds so soon, but I get that."

I shake my head. "It's not just that. I can't put my finger on it."

"It sounds to me like she's got some pretty serious physical concerns going on. You've always had a bit of hero complex, Mateo. Maybe your bat signal senses a damsel in distress?" Max asks.

My first instinct is to deny it but he's right. I've always been the guy who is there when you need help. The guy with the truck to move your shit out of ex's apartment. The guy who will bail you out of jail. The guy who will show up when you call.

I like being that guy. It's hard-wired into my DNA. But when it counted, I failed. Really fucked it all up and let my sister, Mari, and my family down and suddenly I'm not really sure who I am anymore. It doesn't take Dr. Phil to figure out that that I've been dialing it in since then.

Carlisle has her own rules and so do I. They aren't that different: avoid anything where someone can start to depend on you. But Carlisle intrigues me enough to want to dip into the shallow end of that pool again.

"We all know I'm not the guy to rely on," I say.

"Jesus Mateo. Mari would kick your ass if she knew you were' still beating yourself up about it," Max says, his expression equal parts anger and frustration.

"She'd remove his balls if she saw how he's ignoring the medical school stuff that is piling up at our house," Zane adds. I glare at him for outing my procrastination to Max because we both know that when my mom pumps him for info, Max will have to spill. Nobody crosses my mother or lies to her when she asks a question. Carmela Montez Butler takes no shit from anyone, ever.

"Look, that dream of medical school was one I had with Mari. She's gone and I just don't know if it was ever mine."

That is the truth. I don't remember who thought of opening a practice together, helping people one-on-one but I'm not sure it was me. And now... I don't know what the fuck I want or if I have what it takes to do a good job.

"Uh huh. It has *nothing* to do with the fact that you're punishing yourself. Paying some stupid penance." Max doesn't even try to hide his disbelief. "Just get your shit together and go. The only thing Mari wouldn't forgive you throwing away this opportunity."

I'm done with the conversation. My goal is to put off thinking about any of this shit until the day classes begin in a few weeks. If I find myself standing in front of dead guy in Gross Anatomy, then I'll know what I'm going to do.

"Zane are you still playing at that music festival thing in a couple of days?"

If they are surprised by abrupt change in conversation, the only indication is the look that passes between them that I ignore.

"Yeah, why? You coming?"

"Can you get me a spot on the sound stage? Something out of the crowd?"

His face scrunches up into a "what the fuck" face. "Yeah. I can work it out." And then the light bulb goes on and he brushes his long hair out of his face and grins. "You want to treat Carlisle to a little VIP treatment."

I snort and roll my eyes. "She had dinner at the White House, I'm thinking that meeting you backstage is not going to be the highlight of her life." I pull my phone out of pocket. "After today, I'm not sure she can handle standing in huge crowds for all that time."

He nods. "You get her to go and I'll make sure she is well-protected from the 'little people'."

I am able to flip him and hit her number on my phone at the same time. It's a gift.

"You got her number?" Max asks. "I thought she shot you down."

"I took it off the TA list for our class."

"Nice abuse of authority. I like it," Zane says. Of course he does. If there is a rule within five miles, he's breaking it.

The phone rings and I walk out on the balcony just off the bedroom. She picks up on the third ring, laughing with whoever is with her in the background.

"Hello," her voice gets more distant for a second and I envision her checking the caller ID. "Oh wingman. What are you doing? I thought we covered this calling thing this morning."

I smile. Just her voice gets me going and I have to shift to adjust my shorts getting tighter. I need to tread carefully with this woman.

"I was wondering if you want to go see Zane perform the day after tomorrow. Your exam will be done, you will have failed your verbal portion because of your shitty accent and you will need something to distract your from your defeat."

"You suck and you need to stop jinxing me," she laughs.

"You didn't answer my question." I like that I have to chase her a little bit. It's nice for a change.

She sighs. "I told you I don't date."

"And I wasn't asking. The tickets are free and I have an extra. I'm not picking you up, you can meet me there." I pretend to think about her other rules and drag the moment out a bit longer. I can hear her breathing on the other end of the phone; it's a little elevated and I would bet my car that her heart is pounding just like mine. We just do this to each other. "There will be no bed, no sleepover but if you're up for it, I will fuck you."

The sharp inhale from Carlisle ends on a gasp and I know I've got her. It might be the last time we hook up, this thing between us has to burn out sometime, but we'll go out with a bang.

"I don't know how I'm supposed to pass that up," she says, breaking the silence that stretched out a little too long for my comfort. "What time should I meet you?"

"Eight o-clock?"

"Fine. I'll be the one with the cowboy boots and the very low expectations."

I huff out a laugh and hope I can wait to see her. This girl fucking kills me.

"Well, then the only way I can go is up."

Chapter Five

Carlisle

"*Marco?*"

I send the text and look at my phone, waiting for a reply. I'm at the show, held on an outdoor stage in a huge field and there are about twelve gazillion people here. It's dusk, almost dark and I can't tell one writhing, dancing body from another. I am never going to find Mateo in this crowd without a little help.

My phone buzzes in my hand and I look at the screen, so grateful it is backlit and I can see it.

"*Polo*" pops up in the familiar blue text box and I don't have to wait for the direction I need. "*To the left of the sound booth. Back of the audience.*"

I lift my head and scan the area, finding the large sound booth elevated on a small stage and flanked by large light stands. It is on the edge of the crowd of screaming fans listening to a local band play their hearts out. I press forward, circumventing the tight cluster of people and weaving my way around the edges. I feel good tonight, my back is strong but I don't want to get crushed by people having a good time.

"*Marco?*" pops up on my screen and I stop to return the text. "*Polo. Near the t-shirt booth.*"

"*Coming to you. Don't move.*"

I do as I'm told and wait by the stand, watching as people fork over their money for stuff with the music festival logo on the front and a list of all the performers on the back. One guy working behind the counter gives me a curious look but is quickly distracted by the line of people in front of him.

I'm about to send another text when two hands cover my eyes and a rough voice against my ear says, "Marco."

I laugh and turn to face Mateo before answering, "Polo."

He looks down at me, his blue eyes scanning my face and down my body in one hot glance. I look right back and what I see makes my body pulse with the memory of how good it was between us and how much I want to do it again. He's so hot, dressed simply in jeans with a black t-shirt, a ball cap turned backwards on his head. He hasn't shaved today and a dark shadow of hair that I want to reach out and touch covers his jaw.

His eyes spark with the recognition of what I'm thinking, his grin is wide as he leans back in for a quick kiss on my lips and another murmur against my ear. "I've got a spot for us on the sound stage out of the way of the crowd. Zane hooked us up."

I grab his arm, needing to get something out of the way. "Hey."

"Yeah?"

"Thanks again for the other day. It's... " I look around the crowd and consider my words as they stick to the roof of my mouth. "I don't like asking for help." I stumble again. "You were great."

He waves me off. "I get it. What you have to deal with, it sucks. I'm just glad I was there to help out."

"Me too." And I am. "Thanks again."

"Anytime. I'm your wingman, remember?"

His grin is contagious and I nod and take the hand he extends out to me, melting against him when he tugs me close. Mateo parts the crowd, shielding me with his body as we make our way to the sound stage. Once we get there, the security guard at the bottom of the steps nods to Mateo and opens the gate for us to walk up. He leads me to a spot just behind the large table covered with sound equipment where we can lean against the railing and watch the show.

Mateo positions us so that I can rest my weight on the metal rail and moves up behind me, close but not touching as he rests his arms on the railing next to mine. In this position he is all around me, his heat and his scent completely covering me. I like it. I like the sensation that his body has captured mine, that he has no qualm in indulging in the maleness of asserting his dominance and possession in this crowd of people. Anyone who looks at us will know that we've fucked and that we will be doing it again... very soon.

I like it more than I want to but I won't let that deter me from enjoying tonight.

"Is this okay?" he asks, his breath warm on the skin on my neck and I shiver with the goose bumps it raises on my body. He notices my reaction and his groan is low and deep in my ear, moving his hands to link with mine as he leans forward enough to press his chest to my back, his groin into my ass. "Is *this* okay?"

I nod, letting my head fall back to cradle against him and I watch the show. I am not in any hurry to rush to where I know this will end. This is exciting, sexy. I'd forgotten all about this part of the seduction. My time with Aaron seemed so long ago and since him... well, you didn't get much seduction with quick one-offs against a wall or bent over a couch.

I turn my head, brushing my lips along his jaw to ask, "When does Zane go on?"

"After this band."

"Good. I love his stuff. I think I've been to most of his local shows in the last six months."

"Stalker," he teases and pulls away to grab his phone out of his pocket. He thumbs it on and pulls up the camera app. "Let's send him a picture. He was excited when he heard you were coming."

I lean in closer to make sure we get both of our faces in the shot and after a couple of pics that I hope never see the light of day, we get a good one and Mateo leans back against me, circling me in his arms as he types out a quick text and sends the photo.

"So, what did you do today now that classes are officially over?" he asks, brushing his mouth against my ear.

"I helped Livvy pack and mail boxes to New York."

"Ouch. That's going to be rough when she moves, yeah? You guys are really close."

I nod. "Today kind of sucked for both of us. She's excited to finally be with Sarah and I'm happy for her, but I'm going to miss her. She's the first real friend I've had since everything happened."

He's quiet for a few moments and I wonder if he's going to ask me questions about the bombing, about Aaron. Most people do but I realize that he's not drumming up the courage to ask, he's waiting to see if I'm ready to share. I'm not but I'm grateful for his patience.

"I worked out with my trainer. We did weights today and I'm going to feel it in my arms and legs tomorrow," I say.

"That's good. Back injuries require lots of strength training, core work and overall body. Do you swim as part of your routine? The low-impact would be great for you."

"I don't swim anymore." I manage to keep the edge of panic and anger out of my tone but my words still come out like a whip and I feel him tense up at my reaction.

"Ever?"

"No." And I clamp my lips together, unwilling to say more and trying to control the tremor that starts whenever I talk about it.

His phone vibrates in his hand and we both look down. Zane has responded and Mateo quickly presses the screen, both of us relieved to move on from the awkwardness that was creeping into our night.

Zane's sent a selfie, the stage with the current performers in the background of the picture. "*Ariel! Glad you could make it even if you have to hang out with that loser. I'll come find you after the show and rescue you.*"

"He calls me Ariel?" I ask.

Mateo glances at me, his expression a little bit confused. "Yeah. You know the whole red hair and mermaid thing. The swimming… " I keep my expression flat and his words drift off when I don't respond. He's worried about my taking offense. I let the silence drag out a little bit longer before I let him off the hook and smile. His obvious relief makes me laugh out loud.

"Newsflash braintrust, you two aren't the first to think that up." I gesture towards the phone. "Hand it over."

I type onto the screen. *If we fuck, you'll write a song about me. It will go viral. I will have to listen to it for the rest of my life. No thanks. Ariel.*

I hand the phone back to Mateo, noticing for the first time the dark expression on his face. Not anger. Something deeper. Carnal. Something that gets me wet and makes my body flash hot all over.

"I rescind my offer of a threesome. You know this, right?" Mateo pulls me in tight against him, his breath hot against my cheek. "There's no fucking way I can share you with anybody. There would be bloodshed. Prison for me." He punctuates the next few words with a series of small nips against the skin of my neck. "Very. Bad. Idea."

"Well, then you better make my sacrifice worth it." I snake my hand backwards between us, touching as much of his hard abdomen and even harder crotch as I can from my awkward angle.

"You already know I'm worth it. I bet you're already wet for me. Dying for it." He keeps one arm looped around my waist ensuring that I stay where he wants me while the other wanders, skimming over my bare thighs and then inching up under the hem of my denim skirt to trace the bottom curve of an ass cheek. He groans against my ear. "Fuck, I love the fact that you hate underwear."

I lick my lips. "I don't like anything to get in between me and what I want."

He laughs, the sound dark and sensual and the perfect thing to crank me up one notch higher.

"Well, you can't have what you want right now." The tips of his fingers trace the curve of my ass and I hold my breath as he makes a shallow dip into the wet, slick place between my legs. My body sags but he holds me in place in the right spot for him to make me crazy with that dirty mouth.

"If you're a good girl and enjoy Zane's set, later tonight I'll bury my cock in your pussy as deep as you want, for as long as you want, as often as you want. Sound good?"

All I can do is nod and try to get my breathing under control as Mateo removes his fingers from my skirt and wraps both arms around my waist. His phone buzzes in his pocket and I feel it against my hip.

"That's probably Zane. You want to look at it?" I ask.

"Nope. He's getting enough airtime tonight. I want you all to myself."

I'm totally good with that and we remain in that position until Zane is announced and we let go of each other long enough to yell and scream and clap as he comes onstage. The crowd goes absolutely nuts and he reels them in with his sexy banter and the start of his first song. Once again, I'm bowled over with just how good he really is.

"He's awesome," I say to Mateo as we sway together to the music. "Really good. Does he have a record deal yet?"

He shakes his head. "He gets lots of work as a songwriter but he's taking his time picking the label. I think he's waiting until after he goes on tour to pick the one he wants."

"Tour?"

"He's going on tour with Kit Landry as one of her opening acts. His manager thinks he'll get a bigger deal once he's made a splash in major cities."

"How the hell did he get a gig with Kit Landry?" I turn to face him and Mateo stares down at me as if he's trying to decide if I'm joking with him or not. "What? What did I miss?"

"I guess I just figured you knew," he says and grins. "My cousin Max is engaged to Kit. Zane is one of her primary songwriters and we practically live at their house. They feed us and we provide slave labor for all the renovations my cousin insists on doing himself."

"Really? I'm a huge Kit Landry fan."

"Well, I happen to know she's a huge Carlisle Queen fan. I'll introduce you."

I nod as he pulls me into his arms and I loop my arms around his neck. We dance like that for a while as Zane rolls through his set behind us and before I know it, he's done and the next local band is being ushered on stage.

"Let's go."

Mateo takes my hand and leads me down the stairs, nodding at the security guard as we pass by. He places me in front of him, using his larger bulk to part the crowd as we make our way towards the parking area. His hands, heavy on my hips are grounding and sexy at the same time. The slide of our bodies together as we walk in tandem is like blowing air on the smoldering embers of lust we'd lit earlier tonight. It won't take much to get me going. I've been thinking of this since the last time we were together.

"Are we supposed to go catch Zane backstage?" I ask, tilting my head and giving him access as Mateo places soft kisses on my neck. The night is cooling off, not enough to make me cold but the combination of the breeze and his attention is making me shiver, super aware of every inch of my exposed skin.

"No. He'll have plenty of company for the night. Brunette. Blonde." He murmurs against the skin on my shoulder, his teeth tugging gently on the thin strap of my tank top. "I'm partial to redheads at the moment."

"For the moment?"

"Well, I have a very short attention span. Early diagnosis of sexual ADD."

"That sounds serious," I tease, skimming his forearms with my nails and loving the rise of goose bumps on his skin. "What's the cure?"

"I need to get somewhere and focus on my task. Give it my undivided attention for hours."

Getting somewhere and letting him focus on me sounds really, really good. It feels even better when he spins me around, the cool metal of a truck cab against my back and hot, hard male on my front.

He takes my mouth, simple possession with soft lips and

velvet tongue as he coaxes a moan from deep in my throat. I weave my fingers through his hair, pulling him back to me every time he tries to pull away. He tastes of the beer he had during the show, red hot gum, and spicy, half-latino lover.

I travel my hands along the wide expanse of his shoulders, tracing the ripple of defined muscle in his back until I can cup his ass cheeks. Pulling him forward with one rough tug, I grind my pelvis against his hard length and curse the two layers of denim cock blocking me.

I have three brain cells that are not occupied with how I feel right now and it's enough for me to coordinate reaching between our bodies with shaky, sweaty fingers and unfastening the snap and easing the zipper down just far enough for me to feel the heat of him through the fabric of his boxer briefs.

"*Tu Me Vuelves Loca*," he groans against my lips, dipping back in to taste me one more time, his tongue probing in sync with the rhythm of his hips thrusting into my palm. "We need to find somewhere I can get you horizontal."

He doesn't wait for my agreement, although I am completely on board with that plan, and pulls me between the cars parked in orderly rows in a large field. I think this is a farm or something when it isn't hosting a music festival and there are no lights except for the ones aimed at the festival. It gets darker and darker as we move farther from the crowd.

He stops next to his car and pulls me to him for another deep kiss, tongues and teeth and moans from us both. He breaks the kiss long enough to place his hands at my waist and lift me over the door and toss me into the backseat. He's left off the drop top and two seconds later he climbs over the side and joins me in the deep backseat.

"I don't think I can drive right now. You've got me too jacked up," he says. My eyes are adjusted to the darkness and I can see him sprawled against the seat, hair mussed from my hands, lips swollen. The sensitive skin on my neck, my chin and cheeks is tingling from his stubble, and I'm excited by the idea that I might have his marks on me tomorrow. "I feel like

I've been hard for hours."

I glance down at his crotch and can see the outline of his erection through the soft denim, the patch of dark hair above the line of his boxer briefs visible in the "v" of his open fly. I move to straddle him, not lowering myself all the way down, leaving enough room for me to insert my hand under the fabric and stroke his cock. His head thuds back against the seat and he lets out a soft "fuck".

"That's what I want." I lean over, pressing my lips against his so he can feel and hear my words over the music coming from the stage. "I want you to fuck me. Now."

Mateo moves then, his fingers suddenly speared through my hair, forcing me to look at him. He looks as crazed as I feel. This thing between us is bringing out every primal and reckless instinct inside me. Inside both of us.

"People are everywhere. They could see us," he says, his voice ragged with his own need and the effort to verbalize with my fingers wrapped around his penis. "I don't give a shit but I'm an exhibitionist asshole. Are *you* sure?"

"I want it. If you won't do it then I'll find somebody who will."

I think I see an actual flash of blue fire in his eyes at my words. I wouldn't go find someone else when my body is screaming that it only wants him but I remember what he said earlier about not sharing me with anybody as his fingers stroked me. I want *that* possessive, growly guy all over me, inside me, and I will not settle for anything less.

"*Es usted un coño?*" I say, issuing my final challenge.

Chapter Six

Mateo

I can't believe she just asked if I was a pussy.

In the worst accent ever heard.

I know what she's doing. She's pushing my buttons, controlling this scene as much as she can. Classic Carlisle. My control-freak fuck buddy whose lust runs hotter than the red in her hair. Normally, I don't like games. I don't like the push and pull of a mind fuck when I just want to screw a willing body.

But Carlisle's games? Hot. Intriguing. And they make me laugh.

My lips curl up at the corner at the taunt and I bite back a groan at the way her pupils dilate when she realizes she's going to get exactly what she wants and more. I tighten my fingers in her hair, drag her face down to mine and part her lips with a brutal kiss. Her grip on my cock tightens and I buck up into her grasp, aching to feel her touch on my skin.

Carlisle gives back as good as she gets. The nails of her other hand dig into my shoulder and I wince at the spark of pain. It only makes me harder. I let go of her hair, break away from her mouth and drag her tank top straps down to expose her breasts to me. She isn't wearing a bra and I waste no time cupping them both in my palms, dragging my thumbs across the tips.

Her head falls back and she starts with those noises that drove me fucking crazy the last time. Ragged sighs and moans as I stroke her flesh, teasing her pink nipples into hard, tight points. And then she starts with the talking and I wonder if I'm going to come in my pants like I did the first time I ever went down on Erin Delaney in this very car, on this very seat.

"Teo, suck on me. Put them in your mouth."

I want to. Jesus, do I want to do exactly as she commands but I cannot resist teasing her for a little while. I lean forward, making sure my lips skim the curve of her breast, leaving a trail of hot, moist breath as I make my way to her neck. I lick the long column of ivory flesh, nibbling the skin over her pulse point and loving the way she jumps at the contact. I take my time, dragging it out until she grabs my hair in her hands and yanks my head back to force me to look at her.

"Teo. I asked you to suck on my tits. Do it or I will kill you."

I laugh, enjoying the way her eyes narrow even more.

"Go ahead. Get mad," I tease. "It'll only make it hotter."

She growls and pushes my head down to her breasts and I give her what she wants because I'm dying to see her fall apart like she did the other night. Licking, teasing, sucking the hard nubs of flesh into my mouth. I trail my hand down to the space between our bodies and pull up the hem of her short, denim skirt. The scent of her arousal mingles with the summer scent of sunshine baked into earth, fresh-cut grass, and sunscreen to form the most delicious perfume.

My mouth waters and my dick leaks as I slide along the moisture slicking her thighs. She is so wet that my touch glides over her folds as I caress her flesh. She grinds her body down onto my hand, seeking that pressure in the best place possible but I won't let her have it, groaning low in my throat when she whimpers above me. I finally glance a fingertip over her clit and she shudders, her weight collapsing onto me as her legs start to shake.

"Teo, I'm going to come."

I instantly release her nipple from my mouth and remove my hand from her skirt. I lift my hands to frame her face, my voice low and harsh against her ear.

"Don't you dare come right now. I want to drink it up. It's mine and that's how I want it."

"Fuck you," she growls and then her voice goes softer.

"Then take it. Please," she pleads, her nails digging into the muscle of my forearms.

I shift out from under her body, leaving her to face the back of the car, knees resting on the seat, ass up in the air and the top half of her body draped over the back end of the car. Behind her, way off in the distance is the stage, the lightshow making her form look like illuminated abstract art.

I almost choke on my desire as it rises up in my chest and tightens every muscle in my body. I am primed, ready to go. But I want her to go first.

"You look so fucking gorgeous. Everything about you says I can do whatever I want to you and you'll take it."

"Anything you want," she says, her hands clenching and unclenching, gliding over the smooth-as-glass paint job. She demonstrates her submission by spreading her legs wider, her skirt rising to expose the sweet curve of her ass.

I lean down behind her, using my hands to spread her wider, finding her wet folds with my tongue. The first swipe makes her jump but the second has her pushing back against my face. I am beyond teasing at this point. I'm afraid to stroke my own dick because I'm *that close* to coming.

I angle my head and find her clit with my tongue, pressing against it in a rhythm she mimics with her hips. I eat at her, savoring her taste, drinking her arousal as she begins to shiver around me. Her legs shake, her ass muscles clenching under my palm as I caress her silken skin. She's gasping above me, her words lost in the beat of the music as I bring her closer and closer. I don't need to hear them anyway, the way her body goes completely still is what I've been aching for as she comes apart all over my mouth. I continue the pressure, taking her as far as I can, keeping her suspended in her own pleasure until she pulls away, her body collapsing in a boneless heap over the seat.

I rise from my position, pressing kisses along her spine as I drape myself over her body, only stopping when I cover her completely.

"Eres tan bella," I whisper against the damp skin of her

neck, the curls tumbling over her back. I kiss her cheek, trailing down until I can claim her mouth in a soft kiss full of softer sighs and wet tongues. "So beautiful."

"Quiero que me folles," she says, her green eyes flashing with the heat of our unfinished passion.

She wants me to fuck her. No... she's begging me to fuck her.

Her terrible pronunciation does nothing to lessen the impact of her words on my cock. I'm hard, painfully hard, and I want nothing more than to give her what she's asked for.

"I will fuck you." I lean back and pull the condom out of my pocket before shoving my jeans and boxer briefs down to my thighs. The night air is cool against my hot skin but I don't care. Carlisle is running hot enough to burn me alive and I want to be consumed by her tight heat. I rip open the packet and slide it down over my length, leaning forward to slide into her body, her slick lube making it an easy glide forward. She gasps and then lets out a long, satisfied sigh that wraps around my balls. I have to fight the urge to pull out and slam back in. "I will fuck you hard and fast and deep. Are you ready?"

She nods and I pull out almost all the way and then shove my way back in. Carlisle pitches forward with the force of my thrust, throwing out her arms as she spreads herself out on the back of the car again. Her position is open, submissive and I take all she is offering, my hips snapping forward as I move in and out of her wet, willing body.

"Teo. Yes. Yes," she chants over and over, and I fall into a rhythm that brings me closer and closer to my own release. The fire in my lower belly, the ache in my balls tells me that I'm not going to last as long as I want to. That I am not going to be able to resist the tight drag of her sex along my cock, that she will take from me what I am very willing to give to her.

I lean forward, draping my body over her back once again as my thrusts become more and more shallow. I bite the spot where her neck meets her shoulder and she cries out, her hand reaching back and her fingers digging painfully into my hip.

"I need to come," she pants, her words slurred she's so drunk on our lust. "I need... "

"I know what you need," I growl as I wedge my hand between her body and the seat and rub her clit in tandem with my strokes and the heaving jerks of her body under me. "Carlisle, come. I want you to squeeze me tight in your hot little pussy. Come on."

My words and the rutting of my body against hers, pushes her over the edge and I go over with her, my orgasm making me shudder with the white-hot pleasure of it. I hear the music off in the distance but my ears are ringing, blood pulsing through me so fast I can't keep up, even with deep, gulping inhales of the sweet night air. I hold on to her, burying my face in the sweet gardenia scent of her hair, relishing the cool silk of it against my overheated skin.

"Fuck me," she says on a breath that starts out as a sigh and ends on a laugh. "Fuck me."

"Happy to but I need a minute. I'm twenty-two, not Superman."

I lift up and off her body, slowly pressing kisses on any patch of exposed skin I can find. Her skin is like silk against my lips, her taste salty and sweet.

"I could eat you up." I take a quick bite of her ass and tell her just how amazing she is. "You. Are. So. Fucking. Delicious."

We lower ourselves to the seat, a tangle of laughter and limbs. When was the last time I laughed with a lover? Never. Sure, we had a good time. Enjoyed the moment and each other. I didn't stay around or keep them around long enough to laugh together.

But I'm not in any hurry to go anywhere right now. I dispose of the condom, right my clothes and settle lengthwise across the seat, pulling her down alongside of me. The music from the festival continues, providing a perfect backdrop to our silence.

"We need to do that in a bed sometime," I say, tracing a finger up and down her arm. "I'd like to actually see you completely naked."

Carlisle stiffens slightly and I wonder what I've stepped in this time.

"I'm not girlfriend or sleepover material," she answers, her voice soft but firm.

"And I'm not asking you to move in. I'd just like to fuck you, roll over and pretend to sleep while you pick your clothes off the floor and sneak out." I press a kiss against her hair and navigate the land mine field I've clearly landed in. "You can even have a walk of shame."

"You're kind of an asshole."

"I really am but I'd still like to hang out with you again."

"Don't you have medical school or some other time-consuming activity coming up?" She looks up at me, her expression indecipherable but concerned.

"That's the plan." If she's not girlfriend material, I'm not sharing material and that includes my shit about school, my sister, or any of it.

Carlisle remains silent in my arms, the music from the stage drifting over us with the breeze. I get her, I think. She's not cold or stuck-up. A part of her is closed off except when I have my cock buried in her body. The couple of times we've been together, I've seen who she probably was before her body and her life was blown apart and then paraded through the media in the last eighteen months. When something like that happens to you, it is a rare person who can move forward without leaving the old you behind.

"Look, my wingman status remains even if we never fuck again. I'm screwed up and so are you but when I'm fucking you I forget about it for a while. I like sex with you and I like hanging out with you. Nothing more than that." I put a finger under her chin and tip her face up to look at me. Her green eyes are open but clouded with her hesitation. "I don't like to chase women, especially ones who have no desire to be caught. You have my number. You call me when you want to have some fun together. You control it all. Sound good?"

She watches me, her gaze assessing until she rolls her eyes and shakes her head. "Oh hell. You might be a nice guy after all."

I laugh, a little confused. "I try not to be a dick as a general rule but my 'Y' chromosome gets in the way once in a while."

Carlisle laughs, lying back down on my chest. "For the record, I'm not screwed up. I'm okay."

"Really? Okay?" I don't try to hide my skepticism.

"Yep." She nods against my chest before placing a kiss on my collarbone. "And by okay I mean that I'm seriously fucked in the head but I'm sick of talking about it."

Oh hell, this one is just about perfect. I look up at the stars and wonder what I'm doing with this girl.

Chapter Seven

Carlisle

Aaron is in the Student Commons.

Not *actually* Aaron. I'm not having a drug-induced hallucination but my vision blurs a little at the edges and my heart jumps like it's trying to propel itself off the diving block when the race gun goes off. I look around the room and I can't get away from it. His face is on every inadequate-penis-size-compensating flat screen TV in the center displaying either his official summer games photo or live footage of him doing what he did so well.

I try to stand but I can't. It isn't the injury but the surge of nerve-searing pain that shoots from my heart and liquefies every bone in my body. He is beautiful…alive. I stop breathing with the unconscious hope that he will appear, walk right off the screen and into my arms. How many times have I made that silent plea? The wish whispered in the dark to a vast universe that doesn't care about my desire.

I am paralyzed, soaking in his face, his smile. The beard I thought I would hate and then loved. I watch as his long, toned body leaps off the block and slices through the surface of the water. His smiling face as he stands in the center of the awards ceremony, tears of pride running down his cheeks as he salutes our nation's flag. And then the pictures of us together; laughing, kissing, cheering each other on at events start rolling across the screen and the bile rises up from my stomach and I have to breathe again in order to push it back down

The media called us the perfect couple and they didn't know the half of it. Neither of us was easy to live with but we *got* each other the way that only happens if you're lucky. And fuck but we loved each other. Bone-deep and overpowering. I didn't know how lucky we were until he was gone.

And then the footage changes to the carnage, the wreckage of the athlete's village. I close my eyes and dig blindly in my bag for my phone. I didn't need to see the images when I was awake, it would spoil it for when they showed up again in my dreams. My phone is vibrating when I pull it out and I don't even open my eyes to check the caller ID.

"Hello?"

"Is this Carlisle Queen?"

I don't recognize the man's voice and when I glance at the caller ID, I realize that I don't know the number either. I look back up at the TV screen and notice the headline banner at the bottom and suddenly I understand the coverage. The final U.N. report on the bombing has been released and drags up all the memories of the time when that crazy terrorist group tried to send the whole lot of us to hell. I bet my mother's beloved labradoodle that the guy on the other end of my phone is a reporter.

"Ms. Queen? My name is James Moore from the San Francisco Gazette. I was wondering if I could get you reaction to the report—"

I've never been so angry to be right.

I turn off the phone, stand on shaky legs and weave my way in between the tables scattered throughout the room. People are starting to look, their gazes moving like ping pong balls between me and the TV screen and I just keep moving. I'm used to people staring and nobody ignores gawkers better than I do.

My phone rings again and I look at the screen. Another unknown caller. I decline the call, turn off my phone and exit the building heading across the quad. I don't want to wait for the bus and my apartment is only a few blocks away so I start walking. The sunshine is warm on my head and my bare shoulders but my teeth are chattering in spite of the sweat I can feel running down my back and prickling under my arms.

All I can see is Aaron's face. Not the ones where is he is alive and happy but the ones that live in my head. The ones the media will never have because they weren't there. They didn't see what I saw. They didn't taste the blood.

I speed up my steps, wanting to get home before the panic attack I can feel coming on hits me like the bus I narrowly avoid stepping in front of at the corner. I can see my apartment from this location and I scan the area for any news trucks, relieved when I don't see any setting up. They'll be here soon enough, never passing up the chance to ask bullshit questions about the worst day of my life.

I hit the front steps of my building, wishing I could run up them but I get to the front door soon enough. I pull the door behind me to make sure it locks and then I'm pressing the button for the elevator two, four, or seven times. I know it won't make it come any faster but its either that or screaming. I refuse to lose it in the lobby of my building.

I enter the elevator and count off the seconds it takes to get to my floor and then rush down the hallway and unlock my door. I slam the door behind me and toss my purse on the floor, leaning over at the waist with my hands braced on my knees. I struggle to catch my breath, dry heaving as stars flash on the periphery of my vision.

"Oh my God, Carlisle are you okay?" Livvy rushes over to me, her face appearing in in my line of sight as she kneels on the ground in front of me. She raises her hands to cup my face, holding me so that I have to make eye contact. "Breathe. Just breathe with me."

I'm having a panic attack. I've had them before and Livvy has had to coach me through them from time to time. Poor girl, once again I wonder what she did to get stuck with the crazy roommate.

"Carlisle, what happened?" She asks, her face getting some of its color back.

I suck in the air, mimicking her inhale and exhale until I feel my own body regulating itself. I slide down the wall, landing in a heap beside the door. I'm a sweaty, sticky mess but I pull myself together enough to get her up to speed.

"I saw Aaron." I shake my head, knowing I need to start over from the alarmed look she's giving me. ""On TV. They released the final report about the bombing. I've had two reporters call me already."

She jumps up and goes to the window, pulling aside the blinds to look outside. Another perk of living with me, the chance that reporters will camp outside your door.

"I don't see any trucks yet," she says, and turns back to me. "I'll tell my parents that we'll meet at the hotel and not here."

Oh shit. I totally forgot that this is graduation weekend. Perfect.

"I'm so sorry Livvy—"

A sharp knock on the door, followed by a "Carlisle, it's Mateo. Are you in there?"

My stomach does this flip-flop thing at the sound of his voice and I am relieved that he is here. Happy.

I cut a look at Livvy and reach up, turning the door handle and sliding it open. Teo filling up the doorway takes over my view, his face full of concern. He walks inside, shuts the door behind him and drops down to one knee in front of me.

"Jesus, are you okay?" He grabs my hand and frowns. "You're shaking and freezing. What the hell is going on?"

I stare at him, wondering why he is here. I attempt to struggle to my feet and he reaches out and lifts me, holding me against him until I'm steady on my feet. I want to sink into him, steal his warmth and just stay there for about three days. I don't now when it happened but Teo has become something in my life. What I don't really know. Friend. Supporter. Something more.

I don't want him to be anything to me. I don't want to feel the relief that coursed through me when I heard his voice through the door a few moments ago. I'm raw from the photos of Aaron, the wound of my loss is open tonight, too exposed. The fact that Mateo would be any part of healing me is terrifying.

I push him away.

"Carlisle, wait. You're shaking like a leaf and I've never seen you so pale." He looks at Livvy before reaching out for me again. I push him away. "Will you sit down before you face plant on the floor?"

"I'm fine," I insist. I'm stubborn, I know. "I just need a few moments to get myself together.

I walk to the kitchen and pour myself a glass of water, spilling some down the front of my shirt. My hand is shaking so badly that I loose my grip on the glass and it crashes to the counter, shattering and spilling its contents all over the place. I jump back at the same time Mateo and Livvy surge forward to help but I wave them away.

I don't want their help. I don't want them near me.

Livvy grabs a towel and throws it down to stem the tide of the water dripping down on the floor while Mateo pulls me close. His hands cup my face and he does that forehead touching thing that makes me get wobbly in the knees and in the vicinity of my heart and I reach the end of my rope. I want his touch too much. I want his comfort.

I squirm out of his grasp and slide past him, pushing off his hands when he tries to pull me back to him.

"Carlisle, wait... " he says, following me into my room.

"Why are you here Mateo?" I shove my bedroom door open and go to my bathroom. I pull back the mirrored door and pick up the bottle of drugs Dr. Shrieve gave me to take when I have a bad attack. "I open the bottle and shake two onto my palm, dry swallowing them before leaning over to slurp water from the running tap. When I stand upright, Mateo is giving me a weird look in the mirror. "What?"

"I think you take a lots of drugs."

I raise an eyebrow at him as my temper flares. "Do you? I don't remember asking you." I push by him and go out to my room, turning when he grabs my arm. I yank my arm out his grasp. "Get off me!"

"Getting high isn't the answer all the time. I know you

had a terrible thing happen to you but popping pills isn't dealing with it."

I get up in his face, holding nothing back. He gets everything he deserves and I decide to pile on all the shit I'm want to vent to the bombers, the reporters, the doctors. My list is long and my tone is ugly.

"I never asked your opinion about how you think I should deal with being attacked and having the man I love die right in front of me along with some of the best friends I've ever had. I didn't ask for you to comment on the drugs I take or the way I deal with my problems. You are nothing but a fantastic lay and if you think there is anything more than that, you are delusional."

His lips curl up into a sneer and he gives it back as good as I gave it. "You can't function without popping something. Hell, I don't think we've actually fucked without you being high on something. I don't need to be anything to you and I don't expect to be but someone has got to tell you that you are playing a game that you can't possibly win." He points at his chest, his knuckles white he's so tense. "I don't want to turn on the news one day and hear that you overdosed on a bunch of pills and you're gone. Call me nosy or an asshole or whatever but you need to get your shit together and this isn't it."

His words hit a little too close to the mark. His words hurt and I don't need anymore pain right now. I'm done. I just want him gone from my apartment, my life.

"Mateo, you can't fix me. I'm not your goddam Boy Scout project and I just want to you to go. Delete my number. Don't call me. Just go."

He stares at me for what seems like and hour, his jaw tight and blue eyes blazing. He opens his mouth to say one more thing and Livvy interrupts, her tone soft in the midst of all this anger.

"Just go, Mateo. Please."

He transfers his gaze to her and something in her expression deflates him. He nods, never looking at me as he brushes past and leaves my room.

I stand there until I hear him close the front door and then I turn, ready to vent to Livvy about what a judgmental asshole he is. She's standing in the doorway, the look on her face something I can't place. Diappointment? Anger? Hesitation?

"What?" You can't think he was right to say all that shit to me?"

"I think he meant well because he's a nice guy and cares about you but I don't think it was his place." I breathe out a sigh of relief and open my mouth to start the Mateo roast but she keeps talking. "But, I don't think what he said was wrong." She holds up a hand when I rush to argue. "I'm leaving you here and it scares the shit out of me that your normal reaction to any kind of situation is to get high. You had a panic attack and you didn't even try any of the exercises Dr. Shrieve taught you."

"You never said anything before," I say and I am unable to keep the betrayal out of my voice.

"I just did." She steps forward and pulls me into a hug, her body shaking with her emotion. "I know what your plans are and I'll support you with whatever you plan to do in the end. But I love you and I want you to stick around. I'm with Mateo, I don't want to turn on the news anytime soon and I find that I can't call my best friend anymore."

I'm stunned. Speechless, which is a rare situation for me, and with the pills I just took, I'm not reacting as quickly as I want and she's pulling away before I can stop her.

For the second time in less than ten minutes, a person walks out of my room without looking back.

Chapter Eight

Carlisle

The usual crowd is at Mateo and Zane's house.

It isn't a full blown party but there always seems to be a crowd hanging out on the back deck or in the living room playing music or watching a game. This time I find Zane sitting on the patio outside, drinking a beer and strumming guitars with three other guys while a half dozen girls watch them and try to be the one who gets to go home with the musician. I recognize some of them from class but none of their smiles are friendly. I'm the perceived competition and I am the enemy until I am eliminated. Dating these days isn't that different from professional sports.

"Hey Ariel," Zane nods at me as I approach, his smirk knowing and his words coated with "I-knew-this-would-happen" gloating. "You here to patch things up with our boy?"

I'm not getting into my business in front of all these strangers but I nod. "Is he here?"

"In his room," he says and opens his mouth as if he had more to say but then shut it, jerking his chin in the direction of the house.

I walk inside the house and up the stairs, bypassing the people playing Playstation on the couch for Mateo's room. For once in a very long time, I don't regret the fact that my taking them two-at-a-time-days are over. I've got some apologizing to do and like anyone with a healthy ego, it's not a skill set I like using very often. But I was wrong and I need to own up to it.

I knock on his door and wait for the inevitable "fuck off" and I'm not disappointed. His voice is rough, harsh and unwelcoming. Well, this girl is not scared by the Big Bad Wolf routine. It takes more than a grumpy man to send me running…metaphorically, of course.

I turn the doorknob and it slides open and I stick my head in. Mateo is lying on his bed surrounded by a large manila envelope and papers, a beer in one hand and the other tucked behind his head. He's wearing a pair of old camo print shorts and nothing else and I can't help the way my eyes take off on their own journey and travel over the broad width of his chest and the sculpted perfection of his abs. His skin is dark from the early summer sun but I can see the place where his tan line ends peeking out from the open "v" of his unbuttoned shorts.

The dark happy trail entices me to follow its lead and I'm rewarded by the sight of his long expanse of skin broken only by the dusting of dark hair on his pecs and the silken swirl in his armpits. Stubble on his face just elevates his classification from hot to molten and I have to grip the doorknob a little harder to resist the urge to jump his bones.

Instead, I decided to dazzle him with my incredible conversation skills.

"Hey," I say and I have serious doubts about how this is going to end if I can't do any better than that.

He twists his head to the side and gives me the once over before turning back to his original position. "Hey."

"Can I come in?"

"If my telling you to fuck off didn't stop you, I don't know if anything else will work," he grumbles before taking a sip of his beer.

I take that as the only invitation I'm going to get and move fully inside the room, closing the door behind me with a click. The noises from the rest of the house die down to a low rumble and the almost silence in his room is intimidating when I realize that this entire exercise is going to require me to fill it with words. Real words. Not the bullshit you spout at parties or the small talk you make Aunt Irma at Christmas. Real. Fucking. Words.

"Are you going to stand there and ogle me or are you here for a reason?" he asks, his voice muffled by the forearm he now has draped across his face so he can block me out. Nice try. I am completely unembarrassed by the fact that I *was* ogling him not five seconds ago. I bet money he ogles himself too when he looks in a mirror.

I take the four steps it takes to reach his bed, kick off my sandals and climb in next to him. I settle in beside him, lying on my back, so I can look him in the eye if he ever decides to stop hiding.

"You're on my bed."

"I am."

He sighs. "Why are you on my bed?"

"I'm fulfilling one of your deepest fantasies."

That gets his attention and he lowers his arm, his blue eyes narrowed and full of questions. He doesn't look as mad as he was yesterday and I breathe out my own relief.

"I'm admitting I was wrong. I'm sorry," I say.

"You think *that's* my deepest fantasy?" he asks.

"I thought it was every man's fantasy to have a woman admit she was wrong," I say, venturing out with a light smile when he huffs out a tiny laugh and relaxes a little bit. "I'm really sorry. I'm not saying I agree with everything you said but I shouldn't have gone off on you like that. You saw me at my worst, I hope."

He contemplates me for a few seconds, his brain obviously churning with the decision of whether to forgive me or not. I add something hoping to tip him into the "yes" column.

"I'm drug-free today. I had to dodge a few reporters outside my building to come here and I did it buzz-free."

"Really?" He shifts his head on the bed to align better with my line of sight, his eyes searching, examining my face. I try to meet him head-on, to let him see whatever it is he's looking for. Down deep I'm hoping he sees me and it's enough. "Thank you." He pauses before continuing. "You are a lot of fucking trouble Carlisle Queen."

His words make me sad, more than a twinge of regret making me squirm. I settle back against the bed and look at the ceiling. I can feel his gaze still on me, like a touch on my cheek and I can almost hear the questions rolling around in his head. He deserves them, he's helped me out more than anyone lately and I'm ready to share if only to show him that I'm worth all the trouble.

"I was conscious immediately after the bomb went off." I begin in a voice that hurts it is so full of gravel. "I don't remember it going off or throwing me through the air but I remember lying there with pain so bad I threw up." I swallow and feel his fingers lace with my own as he lends me his strength. I soak it in. I need it. "I was walking with Aaron and other athletes, we were going to have dinner. Afterwards, I couldn't find Aaron at first, the smoke was thick and my eyes watered from the chemicals. I was in a lot of pain but I started crawling to find him."

I blink as the ceiling goes blurry and I realize I'm crying, not heavy tears but a steady stream of liquid regret and pain and loss flowing out of me. I don't bother to try and brush them away.

"I found him and I tried to see if he was okay. He wasn't. When I got up close... half his face was missing. His brain... " I suck in a deep breath and force the image out of my head. I couldn't help it if it showed up in my dreams but I didn't have to force it on myself when I was awake. "I draped my body over his and waited to join him. I didn't want him to be alone. The reports from the paramedics and the police said they found me that way. Barely alive myself but protecting him from any other harm."

"You guys took care of each other a lot I guess," he says, tracing a pattern on the back on my palm. It soothes me, grounds me, and I allow myself to accept the comfort. "Two kids so young in such a competitive situation."

"We did. Or at least Aaron tried." I sneak a glance at Mateo, the burn of embarrassment heating my cheeks. "As you know, I'm not good with letting people help me."

"Understatement of the century."

I sigh and squeeze his hand. "I'm working on it."

"Apology accepted. Don't beat yourself up too much about it."

Mateo places his beer on the side table and moves back to me, gathering me in his arms and holding me close as I let the last of the tears flow. His chest is warm and solid and that precious thud of his heartbeat under his skin comforts me. He sifts his fingers through the length of my hair, playing with the strands as he lets me collect myself.

"You are very strong to survive that, Carlisle. I know you don't feel like it all of the time but you are."

I laugh against the wall of muscle beneath me, soaking in his scent and wrapping my arms around him. "I take the drugs to get the shit out of my head that comes rushing back when it all gets to ne too much. If I could erase those images, I wouldn't take anything stronger than the prescriptions I have for pain. Being high turns the movie in my head off for a little while. I'm not sure how strong *that* is."

"I think it's goddam strong," he murmurs and presses a kiss to the top of my head. "I never met Aaron but I think he would agree with me."

I smile at that. These two men couldn't look more different but there is a common core that they share.

"Aaron was strong but it was a quiet power. He wasn't flashy or a trash talker but he gave one-hundred percent everyday and took care of other people. It was a gift and people flocked to it. They trusted him." I peek up at Mateo and catch his gaze to watch his reaction to my words. "You two have that in common."

He rolls his eyes and looks up at the ceiling, shaking his head. "Don't put me on that pedestal. I'll fall off. I promise."

"I doubt that but I'm not trying to put you up that high. It's not your style, at all."

"You think so?"

I shake my head. "You don't strike me as a glory hound guy."

We lie their quiet for a few moments, the sounds of the party below drifting up to us. People are laughing and I can hear Zane and his guitar on the deck.

"You're probably right. Zane's the one who has to have the spotlight to survive. Not that it's a bad thing, just listen to him."

"He seems to have his future all planned out. Fame. Fortune," I say.

"A growing collection of women's underwear thrown at him on stage," Mateo says and I when I look at him to see if he's telling the truth, he nods. "Yeah. He gets panties, thongs, room keys. The worst was a set of dentures with the woman's phone number on them written in Sharpie."

"I think I want to barf."

"It was really gross but Zane said it was good to know that his demographic is cross generational."

"That's one way to look at it."

"He's a half-full kind of guy."

"Mateo, you can't act like you don't have anything special planned. You'll be off at medical school soon." I smack head with the back of my hand, remembering belatedly what happened yesterday. I lean up and kiss him on the cheek. "Happy graduation. I'm embarrassed to say that I don't have a present."

He hugs me close and kisses the end of my nose. "Thanks but this is present enough for me."

"Nice try but I'm getting you a gift. Maybe a stethoscope or a lab coat. Don't you need those things to be a doctor?"

He tenses beside me and I wonder what I've said wrong. I look up him at him but he's staring at the ceiling, his jaw tight and stiff.

"Did I say something wrong?" The silence stretches for a while longer and I decide he's not going to answer me. I've obviously stepped into something major for him. "I'm sorry if I did."

"You didn't say anything wrong, I just don't have any answer for you. I'm not sure I'm even going to medical school. That was a dream I had with my sister Mari and now I don't know if it was ever my dream or if I want it without her."

I think I know the answer but I have to ask. "What happened to Mari?"

"She died. Eighteen months ago," he answers. Six months after I lost Aaron. Rough times all around. "It was a brain tumor. Inoperable. It took her six months from the day she was diagnosed."

He sucks in a wet breath and I keep my eyes down, wanting to give him some privacy to deal with his grief. I understand the need to cry in private.

"I am so sorry. You two were obviously very close."

"We were only eleven months apart and she was my first friend. My best friend. I loved her more than anyone in the world. She was a force of nature." He chuckles and I feel his lips against my temple. "I'm not sure how well you two would have gotten along. Two strong women who are used to getting their way."

"She sounds like she was my kind of girl." I say and I mean it. I've never had any patience for a wilting wallflower. Give me a chick with some thorns any day.

"We were supposed to open a practice together and work with patients one-on-one. The Butler family practice."

"And now you don't know if you want to do it by yourself?"

"Yep." He gestures down to the papers lying beside him on the bed. "This is the paperwork from the school, textbook lists, supplies. I need to make a decision."

"Not that you're asking but I think you should try it out and see if the white lab coat fits before bowing out. You might not actually know until you try it." I think back to my time as a new athlete and the decisions I had to make on the sport I wanted to pursue. "I thought I wanted to be a high diver instead of a swimmer when I began competing."

"What?"

"Yep." I lean up on my elbow and look down on him,

smiling at his surprise. "I went to a few coaches to see if I had any talent for it and they all said no after it became clear that I couldn't do anything more than belly flop."

"So what happened?"

The last coach in Baltimore watched me swim laps one morning. I was on a neighborhood swim team and I was practicing. He said my breaststroke was the best he'd ever seen and that I was like a bullet in the water. I moved from Texas to Baltimore a few months later and the rest was history."

"And twelve medals later... " He pauses and I know what he's going to ask. They all want to know. "Where do you keep your medals?"

"Would you believe that I keep them in my underwear drawer?"

"Is that true?"

I just smile.

Chapter Nine

Mateo

I wake up in fucking heaven.

Carlisle is curled up against me as the little spoon and my dick is rock hard and nestled into the cleft of her ass. Her hair, silky and scented like gardenias is pillowed against my face, surrounding me with a smell I will always associate with Carlisle. I lean up a little bit on my elbow to look down on her and watch her sleep.

I've never seen her so still, so beautiful. Her pale skin has this pinkish glow from the warmth created by our bodies tucked here together in our private cave. I should let her sleep but I can't, I am dying to taste her first thing in the morning, to feel her surrender before she has the chance to put on her armor. I need the real Carlisle and after our talk yesterday, I might have a chance of having her in the early morning light.

My right hand is resting on her hip and I raise it up, lifting her hair away from her neck and giving me access to the smooth column of warm flesh. I start slow, soft. Barely there kisses that she'll feel in her dreams, wonder if they are real, and wake to find her good dreams are just as powerful as her nightmares.

She tastes good, like salt and crème, a sexy woman flavor that gets me even harder. I drift my hand down farther, skating over the curve of her breast underneath her tank top, teasing her nipple through the fabric, It peaks and I groan a little, my mouth watering to get a taste, to feel it roll against my tongue.

I lean over her and ease one strap of her top down over a creamy shoulder and indulge. Reaching out with my tongue, I lick the pebbled flesh watching her fingers curl involuntarily

75

into the sheets below us. The fabric twists between her digits, punctuating the moan that escapes her as I suck her entire nipple into my hot, wet mouth. Suddenly her fingers are digging into my scalp, pressing my face down and encouraging me to continue what I'm doing.

I need no further invitation to nudge her over and off her side until her back is flat against the bed. I stretch out beside her and lean over to suck her other nipple through the flimsy fabric of her top. Carlisle arches up into my touch, begging me with her body and the sounds of want and need pouring out of her to keep going.

I stop and look up to find her gazing down at me, her emerald green eyes dark with her passion, her bottom lip red and swollen from her biting it. I move up, licking along the seam of her lips until she releases her lip from its captivity and I can draw it into mine. I am dying to delve deeper so I abandon her lip to slip my tongue in deep, sweeping alongside her own as it tangles with mine. Her arms are wrapped around my back, pulling me closer as we eat suckle, caress, and explore in the early morning light.

I break off the kiss and look down at her, unable to contain my smile. "I can't believe I finally got you in my bed."

She laughs softly, her fingers stroking the skin at the nape of my next, teasing me with her touch.

"Well, don't waste it. You never know when you'll get me back here."

Her words sober me instantly and dive in for a kiss more bruising and demanding than I intended it to be. I want to claim her, want her to agree that I'm not the only one careening towards a point of no return. Who the fuck am I kidding? We've already passed that point long ago.

I release her mouth and pull back enough to make eye contact. "There is something between us. It's strong and it's not going to go away because we go back to a bunch of rules we made up when we had nothing to lose."

Her eyes go wide and I silently dare her to contradict what I've said, to deny what is pulsing between us like a livewire.

"This could get complicated," she whispers. "It could get messy."

"Like anything between us could be anything else. But I want it. I want you in my bed and in my life."

She doesn't answer and I can see push and pull of what she wants to do and what she thinks she should do waging a war inside her. This is not something either of us signed up for but here we are, right in the middle of it and it feels huge.

"I don't know Mateo, there's so much more you should know… "

"I know that I want you, that I crave being with you in and out of bed and I want to explore it and see where it goes. I'm not asking for you to commit right now but I want you to think about it. Can you do that?"

She nods and I renew our kiss, letting her set the pressure with the way she clutches my head and guides it against her mouth. When she presses down, I obey her silent demand to trail kisses over her jaw, her neck, across her collarbone until I am back at her breasts. I tease with my tongue, little nips of my teeth on one before transferring my attention to the other grinding my hard dick against her thigh as her body writhes and her moans gets louder.

"Carlisle I fucking love it when you lose it. Love how you scream it out, telling me just how good I make you feel."

"Teo, touch me. Come on. Do it," she demands but I'm not ready to give her what she wants yet.

I reach down with my right hand and begin a light caress of the skin of her thighs. She's so hot for me that she reaches down and shimmies her skirt up a bit higher, giving me a glimpse of her auburn landing strip. Carlisle opens her legs wider, her own fingers joining mine on their upward journey, urging them on.

"You want me to touch your pussy Carlisle?"

"Yes."

"Then ask me nicely."

She huffs out a sound somewhere between a laugh and

growl and her eyes snap to mine as she joins our fingers together. "Touch my pussy Teo. Please."

I allow her to drag my hand up and I find her damp, slick and warm. I take her hand and press it against her hot button. "You touch your clit baby and show me how you get yourself off while I finger fuck you."

Carlisle does not break eye contact with me as she does as she's told. I let my gaze drop because I'm dying to see what this looks like. My fingers are darker, blunter as two of them work their way in and out of her body. The sucking pull of her sex on every retreat, as if she doesn't want me to leave.

But the sight of her own, longer delicate fingers rubbing herself in slow circles is enough to get me off if I don't keep control of myself. Her hips shift as she gets closer and I couldn't look away if my life depended on it.

"I'm going to come Teo."

I speed up my thrusts and lean over, nudging her hand to the side as I add my tongue to the mix of sensations. I want to taste her as she comes and it only takes a few tender swipes against her clit and she is shaking under me, her body clutching my fingers in a tight, wet, hot grip.

She tugs on my hair and pulls me up and my mouth is taken in a kiss. She dives in, her tongue going in deep. She wants to taste her on my lips and I let her plunder, enjoying the way she takes what she wants and that what she wants is me.

We break apart, chests heaving with our effort to catch out breath. "I want to fuck you, Carlisle."

"Yes, she nods at the same time her hands start to unfasten the button of on my shorts and ease down the zipper. I'm commando so the next thing I feel is her hand stroking me from root to tip. I shudder when her thumb swipes across the head of my cock and I reach down to still her touch, afraid I might come if she keeps that up.

I lock eyes with her and voice what I've been dreaming about. "I want you naked and underneath me. I have to see you."

***

Carlisle

I freeze at his words. I can't help it.

I have not been entirely naked for a lover since Aaron and the fear that Mateo will be turned off by what he sees flickers across my mind. Normally, I would hedge and find a way to avoid it but this morning, in his bed, with what is pulsing between us, I have to be honest.

"You might not like it." I gesture towards my back. "It's ugly. The surgeons did their best... "

"Let me see," he says, quietly, understanding coating the three words and soothing my fears a little.

I sit up and let him undress me. First my tank top and then my mini-skirt and then I watch hungrily as he gets rid of his shorts. His penis is hard, jutting up against his belly, the tip red and wet. I lick my lips and feel my body clench with wanting him inside me.

"Roll over baby. On your stomach," he whispers and I remember that he will see all of me. I do as he says, there is no turning back now and I lower myself to lie flat against the mattress, open to his scrutiny.

The silence in the room stretches long but I can hear him breathing behind me, his gasp when he sees the mass of scars covering my lower back. I hold my breath.

I expect his touch but what I don't expect is his mouth, pressing soft kisses along every ridge, every keloid, every dip and indent marring my skin. He is straddling my legs, his penis dragging across the skin of my thighs, still hard and urgent and undiminished by the ugliness before his eyes.

Mateo spends long moments examining me, caressing my skin, tracing the evidence of a stranger's hatred with his loving touch and I melt into it. My body relaxes with each passing second and I blink back the prick of tears in my eyes. He moves away for a moment and I hear a drawer open, the ripping of a foil packet and then he is back against me, trailing kisses up my spine until he is draped over me, his breath hot on my cheek.

"Is this okay? " he asks, and when I nod, I feel his cock pressing against my opening. I open my legs sider and we both sigh as he slides inside, full and deep. He stops once he's in, leaning over to capture my mouth in a sweet, deep kiss. "*Tesoro*, you are beautiful. I swear it."

Tesoro. Treasure. Oh fuck, he looks at my broken body and knows what a head case I am and he still thinks I'm a treasure? Holy hell. I can't hear anymore. I'll want to hear more.

"Teo, move, please." I move hips under him, encouraging him. "I need you."

"You don't think you're beautiful, Carlisle?" You think I wouldn't crave doing this if I saw your scars?" He punctuates his word by starting a slow glide in and out of my body. I whimper, the combination of his words and his body, making me crazy and my chest hurt with the way my heart is pounding. "Everything about you is beautiful, gorgeous. I wanted you the first time I saw you and nothing can change that."

I shut my eyes and try to steel my heart against his words. The invasion of my body and the seduction of his words spook me. It's too much and I need him to fuck me and I try to speed things up with my movements but he is having none of it.

"Relax Carlisle, I'm going to give you a slow, deep fuck and you'll believe me by the time I'm done," he murmurs against my ear as he does exactly what he promises. I'm so wet, so turned on that all I can do is writhe under him, welcoming him deeper inside my mind with each thrust of his hips.

Mateo never stops kissing me. My lips, my cheeks, my neck. Always reminding me that he is the one inside, around me. There is no way I can hide in my head and make believe that this is a nameless, faceless fuck. He grounds me to this room and to the time and place and I give in completely when his hands slide up my arms and he covers my hands, linking our fingers together.

"With me, *Tesoro*. Come with me. Come all over me."

I do. It is soft and sweet but erupts electric tingles all over my skin as I fall apart. Mateo is all over me and I have his scent, his sweat, his imprint on me and it is a safe place where I can just revel in my pleasure and his pleasure as he follows me over.

He starts to move off me but I stop him, wanting to keep this closeness, this moment for as long as I possibly can. It is the only way I can explain my agreement to what he suggests next.

"Come home with me today. My parents are having a party and I want you to go with me."

Chapter Ten

Mateo

"I feel like I need to warn you about my mother in advance," I say, looking over at Carlisle in the passenger seat of my car.

I turn on the road in Lively, a little town just outside of Nashville, that leads to the house where I grew up and headed to a BBQ I was dreading until Carlisle said yes. I fully expected her to go home, get cleaned up, change her mind, and cancel on me. So no one was more shocked than me when she appeared in her living room looking like an angel in a long sundress with her hair spilling around her shoulders and a sweet kiss for me.

"I'm actually pretty good with new people. Parents usually like me," she answers. I can't see her eyes behind the sunglasses but her big smile is mocking me.

She has no idea.

We get to the top of the long driveway that leads to the house and I see the small American flags stuck into the ground on each side and I sigh.

"My mom is a naturalized citizen from Cuba. My grandparents escaped and got to Tennessee by way of Florida." I shake my head as the flags get bigger as we get closer to the house. "She is the biggest patriot since George Washington and an even bigger supporter of our teams in the winter and summer games. She screamed when I told her you were coming."

If I hadn't told her I knew I would be the one on the grill, served up later with the baked beans and potato salad. But warning her gave my mom time to prepare for her special guest. I have a pretty good idea of what is going to greet us when we get to the house.

"That is sweet. I can't wait to meet her."

"Sweet is not the word I would use to describe her." As the house comes into view I groan and then laugh at what I see. "I love her but my mom is…intense."

The large, two-story white farmhouse sits in the shelter of tall trees, rose bushes, dogwood, flowering cherry and the flowerbeds my mom has planted over the years. In the few hours since I called, my mom has placed every piece of red, white and blue decorations she has on our house and anything else that can't run away. Bunting, streamers, and flags are everywhere and stretched across the porch is a handmade banner that says "Welcome Carlisle Queen. American champion".

I park at the end of the row of cars and the silence is complete when I turn off the engine. I turn to look at Carlisle and gauge her reaction. Her face is blank and her sunglasses still cover her eyes so it is impossible to know what she is thinking. I watch as she opens the door and steps out of the car, turning in a complete circle to soak it all in.

I start to ask her what she thinks when my mother appears at the side of the house and she makes a beeline for Carlisle who barely has time to remove her sunglasses and brace herself for the arms that pull her into a hug.

"Carlisle! I am so happy to have you in my home. Welcome! Welcome! This is an honor," my mother says in heavily accented English as she continues to squeeze my date like an overly affectionate anaconda. I take a step forward to get Carlisle some breathing room when I see her arms reach up to encircle my mother.

They loosen their hold but do not let go of each other and I stand by and watch as they speak softly to each other, auburn head and darker curls bent together. My mom switches to a mix of Spanish and English as she weaves her words together into a blanket of love and welcome for the newcomer. I can't catch all of it but snatches of their conversation float over to me on the summer wind; words of pride for her accomplishment and sorrow over her loss and, finally, blessings on her future.

This is my mom's superpower, to love everyone with a heart as big as the blue sky open above us. When I was kid I was embarrassed by how my mom was constantly touching people, telling them how special they were, and making sure they were loved. It's why every lonely and neglected friend we had growing up flocked to our house. Carmela Montez Butler never learned to put a filter on her heart.

And I like that she's opened her heart to the woman who is becoming important to me.

My dad strolls up to the scene and pats my shoulder with his big paw of a hand.

"Should we rescue your friend?" he asks.

"I think she's doing fine," I say and turn to look around the yard again. "You got the stuff up quick. I only called a couple of hours ago."

"Kit sent Max over to help so I think you probably owe him more slave labor."

I roll my eyes. "What else is new."

My mom lets go of Carlisle and when they both look at us, their eyelashes are damp.

"Jesus, mom. Did you have to make her cry?" I ask, dodging my mother's swat towards my head.

"Mateo! Do you kiss your *mami* with that mouth?"

"I do and she loves it." I lean over to give her the tainted kiss and glare down at her. "You could have gone easy on her, mom."

"You cannot love in half measures, Mateo. You will know soon enough." She dismisses me with

"It's fine, Teo. It was a good cry." Carlisle gives my mom another squeeze and then turns her smile to my dad. "I'm Carlisle Queen."

"Mike Butler. Welcome to our home," he says, giving her the same shoulder pat he just gave me and then points to the backyard. "I bet you could use a cold drink after meeting my wife…or a nap."

"You can both kiss my *culo*," she grumbles but takes the

hand my dad is holding out to her and follows him towards where the music is playing and the guests are gathered.

"Mom, cursing at me in Spanish is still cursing," I taunt her as I grab Carlisle's hand and follow them. "You doing okay?"

She nods, her smile genuine so I relax. "It was fine. She's pretty awesome really."

"She really is." We round the corner of the house and Carlisle stops me, her gentle "oh" making me smile. "This is where I grew up."

The view in the back is as spectacular as the front. Huge greenspace leading to the man-made lake, barns and outbuildings constructed to match the house and the rolling hills of farmland. I lift my free hand and point to a spot across the lake.

"Straight over there is the farm where my grandparents lived and now belongs to Max and Kit. I have several other cousins who bought other pieces and have built houses on it as well."

"So, as far as I can see, it's Butler land." I nod and she asks, "Do you plan to live here too?

"Not anytime soon but when I do I'll either build on the east side of the lake…" I point out a piece of land to our right. "…or I will live here in this house."

I watch her face as she soaks it all in, pleased that she clearly likes what she sees here. My nervousness about bringing her here is long gone.

"I'm glad you came with me today. Thank you." I lift the hand I am holding to my lips and press a kiss to her knuckles. "I like seeing you here. A lot."

"I like being here. Thanks for inviting me."She leans over and kisses me, soft and sweet and appropriately PG-rated for any age of guest at the party.

I lean back in for another until a voice behind me interrupts us.

"Hey, there are kids around here you know."

Chapter Eleven

Carlisle

Mateo curses against my lips and pulls out of the kiss.

I push down my disappointment and peer around him to see who interrupted my chance for a little bit of sugar. Whoever he is, he resembles Mateo enough for me to presume that this one of the many Butler cousins. He's bulkier but they share the same dark hair and warm smile. I like him immediately.

"Carlisle Queen this is my cousin, Max Butler. Task master and all-around pain in my ass."

I roll my eyes, smiling back as he shakes my hand. "You're the one with the drywall problem." I say.

"My only problem is the assholes who don't know how to put up drywall properly," Max shoots back with a light shove to Mateo's shoulder.

"Holy crap, can't you two act like grown men for two seconds and not embarrass us in front of the special guest?" A tiny woman with red streaks in her dark hair steps between then and they both come to heel pretty quickly. I don't even try to bite back the laugh that bubbles up.

"Aren't you going on tour soon? Mateo asks, draping his arm around her shoulders, trying to intimidate her with his size. She pinches him in the side and he jumps away, rubbing the spot where she made contact. He uses his free hand to gesture between us, making the introductions. "Carlisle Queen this is Kit Landry. Kit Landry this is Carlisle Queen. She has gold medals and you have gold records. Discuss amongst yourselves."

"She has platinum records Mateo," I correct him as I smile at Kit. "I have them all."

"And I am a huge fan of yours as well," Kit says and steps forward to give me a hug. When we step back she cocks her head to the side and looks me up and down. "You're taller than I expected."

"And you're shorter," I answer.

"It's the heels I wear on stage. Everyone says that."

"Everything looks smaller in a competition size pool."

"Ask her where she puts her gold medals," Mateo prompts as the four of us head to a table in the shade. He pulls my chair out for me, his hand lingering on my shoulder as he continues to speak. I love his touch and it would be very easy to get used to it. "She told me she keeps them in her underwear drawer but I don't believe her."

Kit and I lock eyes as she sits down beside me and I wonder if she will guess correctly.

"The real ones are in a safe and the framed replicas are in her closet," she says and I raise my hand to high-five with her. When our palms smack together we both laugh and I decided that I like Kit Landry a whole hell of a lot.

"Wait? Is she right?" Max asks and then looks down at his fiancée. "How did you know that?"

She shrugs and then winks at me. "The real medals are pure silver with gold plating so you aren't going to keep them in a student apartment."

"So far so good," I encourage her to continue.

"And the replicas are in your closet because it feels too braggy to put them in your living room and you don't have an office yet."

"Perfect score," I grin at her and look at Mateo. "Did you really think I kept them in my underwear drawer?"

"People keep all kinds of random stuff in their underwear drawer," he protests.

"Come on genius, let's go get a round of drinks," Max says and moves off in the direction of a group of coolers.

"I'll grab you a water," Mateo says just before he steals a quick kiss and walks away.

"So, how long have you guys been together?" Kit asks

as we settle in to get to know each other better. I hesitate just a little too long and she jumps in. "I didn't mean to put you on the spot. It's just that he doesn't bring dates to family stuff."

"I'm kind of surprised that I'm here actually," I say and wonder how much is oversharing in this situation. "This wasn't supposed to be a thing."

"And now it *is* a thing?"

I think back to our time in bed this morning when Mateo talked about beginnings and what we could be. It's a thing.

"It's gotten complicated really fast."

"Well, that sounds like every great love affair," she teases.

A little girl interrupts with a handful of folded brochures she's placing on each table. I smile at her and pick one up, reading the information on the front for Grace and Peace Hospice Center.

"What is this?" I ask, turning it over and noting it's a facility located in Lively.

"Today is a thank you event for the staff at this hospice center." She pauses and asks, "Did Mateo tell you about Mari?" When I nod she continues. "Carmela volunteers there now but they like to throw a party for the wonderful people who helped Mari and so many other people."

Remembering the kind words she whispered to me just earlier, I am not surprised that Carmela gives her time to a group like this.

"When I was in the hospital and rehab for so many months, there was a group who assisted the families, brought care packages by, and helped with small tasks. My mom said they were a constant source of support." I say, looking over the brochure and reading the testimonials from so many families. "Hospice must have been a comfort. It must have been terrible for them to have her go so quickly."

"She might have had a little more time but she refused any more treatment after her first round of chemo. She was so sick and she didn't want to live what little time she had that way. Mateo was furious with her and they had a huge falling out and never reconciled."

I remember the way Mateo talked about his sister and I cannot imagine him not making it right. "That doesn't sound like the Mateo I know."

"We were all blown away but he just couldn't imagine giving up and not fighting it. He thought she was quitting without fighting and he was furious. When Mari explored assisted suicide options, he just lost it. Max had to drag him out of bars and picked him up in jail once. It was a mess."

"Did she…" I swallow hard to loosen my frozen vocal cords. My grip on the brochure so tight I can feel the paper rip. "Did she go through with it?"

"Her autopsy said that she died from the tumor but I think she did it. Mari was ready and she wanted to go out on her own terms," Kit says, her voice fading as the buzzing in my ears begins to drown out the sounds of the party around us.

Unease spreads over me and gives me a chill even in the heat of the afternoon. Anger is rising fast, aimed at myself and my selfishness in indulging in anything with Mateo. A man whose sister's story is so similar to my own and clearly broke his heart. I had my rules. I broke them. And now I have to make sure that I'm the only one who pays the price.

Chapter Twelve

Carlisle

If I ever meet the guy (or gal) who invented Caller ID, I will kiss them on the mouth.

I glance down at my phone where it buzzes against the couch cushions. Mateo. He's been calling pretty much non-stop since I insisted that he bring me home last night and didn't invite him to stay over. It would have made perfect sense to grab his hand, drag him to bed and let him fuck me until I didn't remember just how screwed up this situation really was. But I just couldn't.

I'd wondered where this connection had come from, why we kept gravitating towards each other and I had my answer now. We are both messed up in the head and everyone knows that opposites attract except when the two people are fucked up. Put two head cases in the same room and they will snap together faster than a virgin's legs on the first date. That had Mateo and me written all over it.

But I'm glad I found out about his sister when I did because that was a recipe for a disaster that would rival the Titanic, Pompeii and Justin Bieber all rolled up together. Our stories aren't identical but the conclusion would be the same: Mateo would end up hurt. I'm not ready to put a name to whatever pulses between us but it's enough of something to make me think twice about continuing it any further. It would be a shitty move and while many would say my plans to check out on my own terms is the ultimate in shitty, I'm not going to drag him any deeper into this when I already suspect that I'm in over my head.

A week of avoiding his calls and he'll have another woman in his bed and *Gross Anatomy* on his mind and I will be forgotten.

The phone alerts me that I have a voicemail and I pick it up, thumbing over the screen to pull up the app. My finger hovers over it and I'd be a liar if I said I wasn't tempted to hear what he has to say. I wouldn't call him back but it would be nice to hear his voice. To see if he is pissed off enough with me for the hint of a Hispanic accent to coat every irritated syllable.

My thighs clench together at the memory of his voice and I moan and it catches in the back of my throat. I swallow hard and try counting to ten to get my heart rate back to a normal level.

I swipe to the left on the screen and press the red "delete" icon when it appears and watch as it removes my temptation. If I'm thinking about listening to his message and *hoping* he has that sexy, southern Spanish drawl thing going on... well... just no.

Mateo Butler is fun and sexy, loves his mother and fixes cars with his dad. He is a guy who helps his grandpa cheat at cornhole and loves his sister so much that her photo displayed on a banner puts tears in his eyes that he doesn't even try to brush away. And then in the ultimate "fuck you" from the universe he's the lover who makes me wet with a heated look and shatters me into a million pieces with his body. He has access to a part of me that's only been touched by one other person; a part I truly thought I'd buried with Aaron.

I'd been wrong.

I consider going to New York to visit Olivia for a week or so. Long enough for things to cool off between us. Long enough for me to forget how it feels to have his weight on top of me, the slide of his rough palm along my body, over my arms, his fingers sliding perfectly into alignment with my own. I knew that staying overnight was a risk. My Achilles Heel was morning sex and when you add to the equation the fact that Mateo is such a great guy, it all adds up to the cost of a plane ticket to JFK.

Am I running? Fuck yeah, I'm running. Because the only

direction my inner compass is pointing me towards at this moment is wherever Mateo Butler was. And I just can't go there. Not anymore.

I open a new tab on my laptop and begin my search for flights. I can leave as early as tomorrow morning if I stick to non-stop in first class. Perfect. I reach for my phone to call Olivia and make sure I can crash at her place. It barely gets to the second ring when she picks up.

"HRH! What's up?"

I smile at her voice, happy to hear the joy across the line. She's loving New York, loving her new job, and head-over-heels for Sarah.

"You sound happy so I guess this means you're not coming back to me."

"Sorry babe, you've got all the right equipment but my heart belongs to another."

I laugh, settling back against the couch, suddenly so glad that I called her. I miss her. She's my best friend and I send up a silent thank you to the heavens that she answered my ad for a roommate all those months ago. She was strange, hard to impress, and even harder to love. We were a perfect match.

"If I didn't love you so much, I'd write bad things about you on the bathroom wall."

"That's not really a threat since they'd all be true."

"I'll tell them you like dick," I tease.

"Oh, that's low even for you," she chuckles on her end of the phone and I can hear the sounds of the city in the background. "I'm late for work so I gotta cut this foreplay short princess. What's up?"

"Can I come hang out with you and Sarah for a little while? A few days? A week, tops." They are still in the honeymoon phase of finally living together again after two long years apart and I don't want to cramp their style for too long.

"Sure. Stay as long as you want." She does something on her end that makes her voice fade a little but I hear her question. "When will you be here?"

"I was thinking of flying out tomorrow morning."

She stops. I can't see it but I know she has by the swift inhale that travels over the line.

"Carlisle, are you okay?"

I kick myself for putting the fear in her voice. If she's using my real name, I know she's freaking out. "I'm fine. I'm still going to set off every metal detector I get near at the airport but I'm fine."

"No. You're not."

I sigh and throw her as much of the bone as I want to send over the line. "It's nothing physical. I need to see my best friend, eat pounds of frozen cookie dough, and watch an Avengers marathon."

She sighs. "Fuck. It's Mateo Butler isn't it?" And then all traces of nice leaves her voice and the chill in her tone makes me shiver. "Did he hurt you?"

"No. No, it's not that."

"But this is about him. I'm right. Yes?" When I don't answer she demands, "What's going on?"

"He's a *nice guy*, Livvie."

Her pause is filled with horns honking and the bustle created by millions of people crammed on an island and I count off the seconds until she responds, her voice low and a little shocked.

"Well, that fucking sucks."

"Yeah. It does." I take a deep breath and try to inject something other than the panic I am feeling in my response. "So, can I come stay with you guys?"

"Stay as long as you want. Just get here already."

"Tommorrow. I'll text you my flight details."

We say our goodbyes and I end the call, settling back against the couch to think about what I need to do in order to be gone a week or maybe two. With no classes, I can zip down to Texas and see my parents. The last time I talked to my mom she'd laid on the guilt pretty thick and I need to go see them or they will come here.

My phone buzzes again and I look at the Caller ID,

smiling at the name flashing on the screen. Speak of the devil.

"Hey mom. That's weird, I was just thinking—" I stop when I hear her clearly crying on the other end of the line and my stomach churns with icy hot fear. "What's wrong? Is it Andrew?"

With my older brother serving in the Marines overseas, I hate that my mind always goes to the worst case scenario but I know first-hand just how very breakable we all are.

"No," she manages to say through the sniffles. "Andrew and Dad. Everybody's fine."

I let up on the death grip I have on my phone and stand up, heading to the kitchen to grab a soda from the fridge. I yank the door open and snag one of the glass bottles that hold my favorite local root beer. I pop off the cap with the opener and take my first sip while I wait for my mom to pull herself together. She's not a crier. April Queen is the one who kicked my ass when I didn't want to get up and go train, who protected me from all the crazy that happens when your kid is a world-class athlete at thirteen, and the one who held our family together when I was hurt, so I know that whatever this is…it's something worth crying about.

"Mom. You're freaking me out."

"I'm sorry Carlisle but it's the most incredible news." Her voice is muffled and I realize that she's talking to my dad. The phone makes a weird clicking sound and the abundance of background noise tells me that I'm on speakerphone. "We got the most amazing call today from Dr. Bertrand's office."

Dr. Bertrand? Who the hell is he… or she? I've seen a million doctors on every freakin' continent since I was hurt and I gave up keeping track a long time ago.

"Mom, I have no idea who that is."

"He's the doctor who can do the surgery you need to remove all of the shrapnel."

That stops me. I know exactly who she's talking about now. This Bertrand guy is the doctor of all doctors who can do this intricate type of spinal surgery to take all of the metal out of my body. If he does this, then the chance of this killing me disappears but there is a high likelihood that I will emerge from the surgery with some level of limited mobility. I could end up using only crutches after months of physical therapy but there is a higher chance I will be a paraplegic. Wheelchair bound for the rest of my life. I feel queasy and I out the soda down on the counter.

I barely register that I am asking follow-up questions. "He said he wouldn't do it. What changed his mind?"

"He looked at your latest x-rays and MRI's and thinks you're a perfect candidate. He's prepared to do it as early as next week. Isn't that wonderful news?"

"I don't know."

"What do you mean you don't know? This is the chance for you to live a long, happy life," my mom responds, her voice flattened by her confusion. "You aren't thinking of not having the surgery are you because that would be crazy. Selfish."

"I don't want to live my life as a paraplegic. I don't think I can." I sigh. "I've told you this before. That is not what I want."

"I don't understand," my dad says, his deep voice booming over the phone. "Are you saying you would rather die than be in a wheelchair?"

"I would, yes."

My parents go silent on the other end of the phone and I wonder if we got disconnected until I hear my dad's voice, low and soothing and the unmistakable sound of my mom crying.

"Mom, don't cry," I plead, knowing it will not work.

"I prayed for this... " Her voice breaks but she pulls herself together enough to scold me. "I prayed for this miracle and you're telling me you don't want it?"

"Not if it is going to condemn me to a life I do not want to live." I struggle to gather my thoughts will all the things pinging in my brain like a pinball machine. I don't want to hurt them but I don't know how I can do that and still tell them the truth. "I've lost enough already. I should get to choose how this all ends."

The voice that rings out in my ear is the one that made coaches weep and cower in the corner. April Queen was the fiercest mom in competitive sports. Nobody even looked at me sideways without her defending me, my training time, my opportunity. I saw the biggest, baddest coaches and sports professionals duck around the corner to hide when they knew they'd wandered into the crosshairs of my mom.

Dr. Bertrand held out longer than the rest and the last "no" he delivered to us sounded pretty final to me. Apparently, my mother didn't take no for an answer.

And she isn't going to take it now either.

I hear my mother take the call off speaker and pick it up. Her voice is firm, immovable. "I'm flying out in two days to help you get ready for the surgery. He wants to do this next week and you will have it. This is not up for discussion Carlisle. I will not stand by and let you kill yourself by failing to act."

She hangs up before I can tell her that I am planning to act quite decisively if it comes down to it. She wouldn't hear me anyway. My mom has made it her life to track down any and every doctor in the universe who could help me. I'm beyond grateful. I'm still walking around because she kept pushing and persuading and harassing every medical professional to look at my case and do something.

And it will take a face-to-face argument to change her mind now.

I sit on one of my barstools and let it sink in. I've been living with a death sentence hanging over my head for so long I don't really know how to feel. I gave up hoping for a reprieve so long ago that my plans to go out on my own terms was an old friend. Comfortable and predictable.

But this change, this chance, is scary and unknown and out of my control. If I have the surgery, I will have a long lifetime of shit to think about and plan and do. A life that can include so many things I'd pushed off my menu because I was never going to get the chance to order.

Now I have an all-you-can-eat-buffet spread out in front of me and instead of falling on the table and gobbling it all up I've lost my appetite. I'm numb because of something burning in my chest that feels a lot like hope and a yearning for one person.

And it scares the shit out of me because the first person I thought of when my mom broke the news was Mateo. If I have the surgery, I could have more time with him. We could be something beyond friendly fuck buddies.

I can stick around... for him.

This is too much for my brain to process. Full blown panic leaves the taste of acid in my mouth and I know I cannot stay here right now. I slide off the stool and stumble for my purse but simply dump the contents on the counter when the tremor in my hands prevents my fingers from working properly. I spy what I'm looking for and manage to get the Molly out of the envelope, washing it down with what is left of my root beer.

I toss my wallet, my keys and my phone back into the bag and head for the door. Tonight I want to be with a crowd of strangers and not think for a while.

Luckily, I know just the place to go.

Chapter Thirteen

Mateo

My phone rings and I pick it up on the third or fourth ring.

I look at the display. Zane. He's got a show tonight at Toot's, a big semi-dive place in town that caters to a rougher crowd who like good music, hard liquor and a really good time. It also has frequents nights where a brawl breaks out and the cops have to come out and sort through the drunks and assholes. I really hope tonight isn't one of those nights because I don't want to make a trip to the police station tonight.

"What the fuck, Zane?" I growl into the phone. "I don't have any money for bail."

"Mateo listen up, all I've got is a few minutes in between sets." He's shouting a little over the noise in the background but I hear him loud and clear. "Your girl is here and she's pretty fucked up."

I want to remind him that she's not my girl. Being my girl would require her to pick up my phone calls or answer my texts. Carlisle Queen has been radio silent since I dropped her off at her house and she didn't invite me up.

But Zane sounds spooked and suddenly the Facebook status of our relationship is all background noise.

"I'm on my way."

I dress and jump in my car, breaking several moving violations to get to Toot's as quickly as possible. I pull my car into the gravel lot and park with a move that would make Bo and Luke Duke proud and I run to the building.

I get to the door and pay the cover charge and begin the process of elbowing my way through a pretty big crowd of drunk people. The bar smells of booze, sweat, too much perfume, and the desperation of people who realize it's about an hour from last call.

It isn't easy to push through and I get more than one nasty look but I'm on a mission to find Carlisle before she does something dumb. Or something dumber than coming to Toot's by herself.

I make my way to the stage and Zane is front and center, belting out a cover of a popular song and wailing on his guitar. I move forward and get as close as I can to the stage with the Zane groupies all lined up on the edge and trying to get his attention with their "pick me, pick me" boob displays. I start to wave to get his attention but he's got an eye out for me and he points towards the left side of the room, never breaking stride on the lyrics or the chords.

I twist around and I see her, the red hair is like a beacon even in the dark haze of the room. I also have her location hard-wired into my body like it's GPS. She's dancing on the floor by herself, which is good, but she's got an audience of three or four huge guys who could easily get work as extras on "Sons of Anarchy". Fuck me.

I shove my way through the crowds pretty quickly, only allowing myself to breathe when I have my hands on her.

"Carlisle!" I shout over the music while I do a quick once-over of her body. She looks fine but she's not dressed for a night out. Jeans and t-shirt with her red and white chucks are not pick-me-up-and-take-me-home clothes and I let go of the pit in the bottom of my stomach. "Carlisle, we've got to go."

"Mateo!" Her smile is bright, her pupils blown and she is swaying in time with music from another bar because it doesn't even remotely match the beat of Zane's song. She's hopped up on something and I'm guessing it's her favorite party friend, Molly. Jesus.

"Babe, we've got to get you out of here." She nods happily and I send up a prayer that her drug of choice makes her very agreeable because I don't have time to deal with her and the three big biker guys who have moved in our direction.

They look like a group of dogs who are seriously pissed that I just took away their favorite chew toy.

"Hey," the big guy in the middle shouts at me. "We were here first."

Fuck me. I'm going to kick her ass when she sobers up tomorrow. I swear to God.

I'm not crazy enough to take on three guys at once. I might do stupid stuff but I don't have a death wish. What I *do have* is years of experience on what can turn a guy off as fast as he got turned on in the first place. I use the first thing that comes to mind.

"She's underage!" I yell and then I put a cherry on that banana-bullshit-split. "Her dad's a cop and he'll kill me if he knows she was here."

I guess their prison experience wasn't something they want to repeat because they back off pretty quickly and I start moving Carlisle out of this place before the last call stampede begins. Even with her being so compliant, it's difficult to maneuver her through the crowd and when I see her wince in pain when she's jostled by a group of happy drunks, I do what I have to do.

"Hang on to my neck," I shout in her ear and I bend down and pick her up in my arms.

I look like Richard Gere in "An Officer and a Gentleman" when he takes Debra Winger away from her crappy factory job and I feel ridiculous. But it parts the crowds before us and I walk us out the front door of Toot's and get her in my car without incident. I slide behind the wheel and send a quick thank you text to Zane and tell him that I'll be at Carlisle's place.

I glance over at the passenger seat and she's out cold, snoring softly as if this is something that happens to her every day. I worry that this is a state she is in every day but since the last time I brought it up I got my ass handed to me, I'll keep it to myself.

The crowd is starting to grow in the parking lot and I don't want to be here when all the drunks try to leave at one time. I start the car and drive back to her apartment, glancing over at her often to make sure she's okay.

Traffic is light and it takes no time to get to her place and when I can't wake her up I have to execute the same move I did in the club to get her inside. It would be way easier to place her in a fireman's hold but with her back injury, I worry that I will hurt her. So I navigate the steps and the old elevator and finally get to her door.

I dig her keys out of her purse and get us inside and take her straight to bed. I pull off her chucks, leave on everything else and pull the covers over her. I sit beside her on the bed and brush her hair back from her face, letting the red gold satin caress the back of my hand. I watch her sleep and wonder just what the hell is going on in her head.

Carlisle Queen is beautiful and sexy and funny and seriously fucked up. I should leave her alone but I can't. Somewhere in the middle of the sex and the drugs and the things that neither of us like to talk about, I started falling for her.

I stand and kick off my shoes and climb into bed beside her, tugging her over until her cheek rests against my chest and I can feel the steady rise and fall of her breathing, the warmth of her length pressed against mine.

I know better than anyone that I'm not the guy she's going to need. My track record for sticking when things go to shit is phenomenally bad. I couldn't do it for my sister. I don't know if I can do it for Carlisle.

But the truth is that when she needs me, even if she doesn't ask for it, I answer the bat signal. Every. Damn. Time.

And that has to mean something.

Chapter Fourteen

Carlisle

"I know we call you Ariel but right now you look a lot like Sleeping Beauty."

I blink at the morning light streaming through my bedroom window and curl into the warm body pressed against me in my bed. I don't need to look up at his face to know that it's Teo. His smell, the muscles underneath his clothes, the way he holds me under the reassuring weight of his arm are well known to me, branded into my muscle memory.

I just don't know how he got here.

"How did you get here?" I ask, moving to the side as he stretches beside me. His dark hair is messed up in that sexy way I like and his stubble is dark on his jaw and makes his blue eyes stand out.

"Zane called me and told me that you were at Toot's having too much fun so I brought you home."

Last night is a blur of music and dancing and forgetting all about the phone call from my mom. I headed straight to Toot's. I knew Zane was playing so I was guaranteed a good show to provide a few hours of distraction. The crowd there is always a bit rough but friendly enough. I had a good time. Mission accomplished.

"Too much fun? No such thing." I wave him off, avoiding eye contact as I gingerly make my way out of the bed. I test the leg cooperation this morning and besides the stiffness that always is around in the morning I feel pretty good. I also feel Mateo's eyes on me and I stand, escaping to the shield of my bathroom.

He's not supposed to be here. I'm avoiding him for a

very good reason and now I really don't need to drag him into all this mess. I need to get him out of my apartment.

I grab my toothbrush and squeeze out a generous dollop and begin the process of removing the nasty scum from my teeth. My reflection is nothing much to look at; my hair is in a tangled snarl, and the mascara smudged below my eyes makes me look like a deranged raccoon. Mateo appears in my side view, leaning against the doorframe, his sexy, lanky length tempting me to give him the slow once-over or to drag him back to bed and get all those clothes off of him.

He quirks an eyebrow at me as if he knows what I'm thinking and it pisses me off. I bend over, turn on the water and spit in the sink. I try to move past him but he stops me with an arm across the opening.

"Extra toothbrush?"

I lean back, pull open a drawer and locate a spare toothbrush my dentist gave me at my last appointment and hand it over. He takes it with the hand stretched across the door and we stare at each other for a few moments before he finally lowers his arm and lets me pass.

"I take it back," he calls after me. "You're more like the princess and the pea. In a shitty ass mood after sleeping on a boulder all night."

I ignore him and head to the kitchen where I put on a pot of coffee and stare at it while it begins to brew. I know Mateo isn't going to cooperate and just leave without talking about why I was at Toot's last night. If I talk about last night then everything will come out and I just can't handle it all if he knows. I care about what he thinks. I care about hurting him. I care about him.

He strides into the room and walks over to the coffee pot, pours a mug and settles back against the counter and stares at me. I can feel his eyes shoot laser beams into the back of my head and I resist the urge to actually flinch. I am so aware of him when he is in the room that it feels like a palpable touch. One more data point to prove that Mateo means too much to me.

"I get that we're done. You don't want me to call, you don't want me in your bed anymore. Fine. But you need to tell me why you were at Toot's last night. Alone. High," he demands, his voice low but angry.

"I wanted to go out."

"To *that* place? Alone?"

"I wanted to see Zane play and I've been to Toot's before. It was just another night out."

He lets out a frustrated sigh that tells me he's reaching the end of his patience with me. "Carlisle, you need to start talking because you're not stupid and you're not foolish so I don't understand why I found you in that bar high as a fucking kite."

I walk out of the kitchen and into my living room, taking a seat on the sofa. Mateo follows me, seating himself directly in my line of sight. He's gritting his teeth, pissed off and not even trying to hide it.

"I'm not trying to be a dick but I almost got my ass kicked last night by three very big guys who have likely done prison time. I get that something happened and you are done with me but I care about you and I need you to answer my question." He slams down his coffee and it splashes all over the table and his hand. It's still molten hot but he doesn't even flinch. "Do you have a death wish or something I don't know about?"

I freeze at his question, my blood and skin tingling with how close he's come to tapping into my brain. I am too slow to hide my reaction but I can see his clearly. I never understood it when books said that the blood drained from someone's face with shock but I do now.

"Carlisle." He swallows hard, his speech stilted as he chooses his words carefully. "Do you want to kill yourself?"

And then I realize that if I care about him at all, I need to tell him the truth.

"I need to explain—" I try to answer him but he cuts me off.

"What is there to explain? I cannot understand this at

all." I put my coffee down on the table and move to sit closer to him. I reach out to touch him but he pulls away and I feel like I'm losing something vital. Elemental. "Don't touch me."

"Okay." I deserve his rejection and the venom in his voice and even though it kills me to see the pain and confusion in his eyes, I maintain eye contact. "You know that I have shrapnel in my back that surgeons could not remove. What you don't know is that if I leave it in my body it will paralyze or kill me."

"Jesus," he says, his shoulders slumping with the weight of my words. A burden I never wanted to give him.

"There is one guy in the whole world who can do the surgery that gets it all out and not kill me on the table but he refused to do it…until yesterday." Mateo's expression immediately lightens and the hope in his eyes makes my heart hurt. I can't let him think this is a viable option. "I don't want to have the surgery."

"What? Why?"

"If he does the surgery I will have some level of limited mobility. I could walk with crutches or I could be paralyzed from the waist down and be confined to a wheelchair."

"But if you don't have the surgery you could die," Mateo counters and I know the exact moment he understands what I have planned to do. Horror, stark and ugly, mixed with disbelief twists his lips into a grimace. He stands, his entire body shaking with his outrage. "You'd rather *die*?"

"I'd rather live…just not in a wheelchair."

"That's so selfish," he accuses. "What about your parents? Livvy?" He lifts his hand and pounds it against his chest, each hard thump punctuating his words. "*What about me?*"

I break eye contact with him but he's having none of it. Mateo drops to kneel in front of me and lifts my face to meet his gaze. He's in pain. I can feel it rolling off him in waves and I have to reach out and touch him, caressing his face with my open palm. He nuzzles into me and my breath catches, my heart squeezing painfully.

"Don't ask me that Mateo."

"You knew you were going to do this and you got involved with me anyway?"

"I didn't mean to. I kept thinking we were keeping it light or I was the only one getting in too deep." I lean my forehead against his and close my eyes. He leans into the touch like he always does, rubbing our noses together, lips brushing with the lightness of a butterfly. "I didn't know it would happen so fast and when I heard about Mari, I knew it had to end. I'm so sorry. I never meant to hurt you."

We sit like that for several long moments and I memorize his strength, his warmth, the pure pleasure of his touch.

"Mateo, I went too far. I was not fair to you when I began this or when I kept it going. And I want to tell myself to have the surgery so that we could have this for longer and see what it could be. It is enticing and you are the dream I didn't even know I wanted anymore. But I can't make this decision for you or my parents or my friends. It needs to be a decision I can live with no matter what happens in the end."

He pulls away from me and I have to sit on my hands to resist the urge to pull him back and wrap myself around him. I can't ask him to do this for me when I can't return the favor.

"Well, then you'll understand I can't sit around and watch you choose to die," his voice is wet with his emotion and it sparks the tears spilling down over my cheeks. "I did it before and I just can't do it again. I'm sorry Carlisle."

I watch as he walks to the door, opens it, and leaves.

He doesn't look back.

Chapter Fifteen

Carlisle

"Dr. Shrieve, you have to tell me what to do."

"Carlisle, that's not how it works and you know it," she says from her usual chair. She's not dressed in her usual psychiatrist outfit but wearing jeans and a t-shirt from the last Miranda Lambert tour. I guess she doesn't bother to worry about her clothes when her patient calls after hours for an emergency appointment.

"I'm paying you double your rate and you're going to play shrink head games with me?"

"Carlisle, I can't make this decision for you. Nobody can." She puts down the notebooks and leans her arms on her elbows. "It is your body and your future and you are the one who has to live with the consequences. I'm here to help you make the decision for yourself."

"But, I don't know what I want. My parents want me to have the operation." I stand and pace the room, unable to sit while my gut is churning like an ice cream machine set on flash freeze. "Mateo wants me to have the operation. Livvy wants me to have the operation. If I make any other choice I let them all down."

"Okay, let's walk through your options. You already made the decision to take your life. If you don't have the operation you will have the same outcome. The only difference is that they know and will have to stand by and watch you do it and you will have to witness the impact your death would have on them. Correct?"

I nod and she's continues.

"If you have the operation, you live. Maybe in a wheelchair, maybe with crutches but you live. You'll have months of rehab and will need help and we both know how much you hate asking for help. But, you will have your whole like ahead of you to whatever you want. Stay in school. Drop out. Compete again. Move to Tasmania. The possibilities are endless."

And that is what terrifies me.

"I got used to only having to plan for a short period of time. Time where I could live like I wanted to live," I whisper, my mouth dry and throat sore.

"Carlisle, can I tell you what I think has you so scared?" I sit and nod at her, my entire focus on the woman I hop can make sense of all the threads tangled in my head. "I never thought I would see you even contemplate changing your mind. Your death, the timing, the way you were going to do it was all under your control. There were very few variables to surprise you." She takes off her glasses and places them on the table, for the first time in our entire relationship moving to sit next to me on the sofa. "When those people murdered Aaron and your friends they also took your control and that scared you. It would scare anyone. Suddenly, the world you had owned and ordered to your satisfaction was gone and it was at the whim of people you never met. Your perspective shifted and now the world was a big scary place where nothing was guaranteed, nothing was safe and there was nothing you could do about it."

Dr. Shrieve reaches over to the table and picks up the tissue box, handing it to me. I take one and wipe my face, surprised when it comes back wet.

"I've cried more in the last fucking week than I've cried since the bombing," I complain, swiping angrily at the tears.

"And I think your body is telling you that you need to so go with it. Let it happen. Stop holding on so tight." She pats my hand and asks. "Are you ready to hear more?"

"Yes, please."

"Hope is the belief that things in the future will work out for the best and they took that from you. So, for you there was nothing worth staying for, no reason to believe that the future would be any better than the past. But now you have things in your life that make you hope and taking your life isn't the only option. I think it's the reason why you didn't tell your mom no and I think it's why you called me."

I remember the moment my mom told me and the way that Mateo flashed in my mind. I

"But I can't make this decision based on people who may or may not be there. I lost Aaron and I don't know if I can live through that again. I don't want to love that way again. It's terrifying."

"Because they might leave or die?"

"Yes!"

"Well, welcome back to the human race, Carlisle. Join the terrifying adventure of love and life that the rest of have to endure. A journey that is only worth making because of the people we love along the way even though we know we could lose them." She reaches out and grabs my hand. "Embrace your hope again and decide if the future might be worth it no matter who comes or goes. There are so many things you will never be able to control but if you're the Carlisle Queen that *I know*, you'll wring out every ounce of adventure no matter what life throws at you."

And just like that, I know what I'm going to do.

Chapter Sixteen

Mateo

I went home.

College graduate. Grown ass man. I'd lasted one long, sleepless night in my house before I got in my car and headed home to my mom. My dad, actually. Carmela Montez Butler could be all kinds of sweetness, light and homemade cookies when necessary, but in this instance I knew what she would do. My mom would smack me upside the back of my head, tell me to get that exact body part out of my butt and head on back to Carlisle's house. She is the call-to-action part of our family, the one who believes that making lists and getting busy is the best way to get the shit in your head straight.

My dad, is the thinker. The listener. The one who patiently coaxes an answer out of you just like he gets every beat up car that rolls into his shop to purr like a kitten and shine brighter than a Victoria's Secret model on the runway.

And right now I need somebody to help me sort out all the crap in my head because I sure as hell can't do it myself. Maybe if I can get my brain straight, the ice in my veins will thaw and the shards of glass in my gut will disappear.

I pull into the gravel driveway tucked under the shade trees in the side yard and head for the garage tucked behind the barn on the back of our property. It is his place, his man cave long before there were TV shows about it. Instead of large flat screens and beer taps, my dad is happy with a set of hydraulic lifts and the smell of engine grease. I find him in his usual position, shoulders deep in the front end of an old car with an old-fashioned country station on the radio.

He looks up when I walk through the door, delivering his usual "Hey Son" in that deep, rumbling voice that can either soothe or strike terror in anyone within a five-mile radius. Something on my face makes him straighten up to his full height of six-feet three-inches and before I know it, he grabs me and pulls me into his arms. My dad isn't a hugger; more of the type to slap you on the back or place a heavy palm on your shoulder and I can count on two hands the number of times he's given me a hug since I hit puberty.

But he holds me now, letting my anger and grief and frustration leech out of me and dampen the front of his shirt.

"She's dying, Dad."

His arms tighten around me at my words and I burrow a little closer, grateful to hide my face against his shoulder as I give in to the panic and the teeth-chattering terror that squeezes me in its cruel grip. Gradually I calm down and pull out of his embrace, wiping my face with the hem of my t-shirt. I avoid meeting his eyes, embarrassed at the way I've completely fallen apart.

He says nothing, instead he does what he always does and walks back to the open hood of the car and reaches for a tool, handing it over to me. I take it from him, the wrench cool against the skin of my palm. I glance up at him and he barely makes eye contact before he gestures towards the engine. I know what he wants me to do, I've spent as much time in the garage as I have in school, or on the football field, or the backseat of my car with a naked girl.

I begin the methodical process of reconnecting wires and hoses, letting the familiar actions work their magic to settle my nerves and kick my brain back into the zone of normal. We work side-by-side for half an hour before he says anything.

"Why don't you tell me what's wrong with your girl?"

"There's shrapnel in her back from the bombing," I say, trying to quickly capture the basics of what Carlisle relayed to me last night. I hadn't caught it all. Not with the shock and the prior night's lack of sleep but the most important parts are cemented in my mind. "It's been in there causing more damage to her spinal cord and one day, very soon, it is going to paralyze her or... " I suck in a breath and force out the words that feel like razor blades in my throat, "... or it's going to kill her."

My dad stops what he is doing and looks at me, the steel gray in his eyes one of the things I know I inherited from him, along with my stubborn streak and hopefully his patience.

"They can't do anything for her?" he asks.

"There's an operation... nobody has been willing to do it until now... "

"But now somebody will do it. Yes?"

"Yes," I say, putting down the tools. My hands are shaking too hard to use them properly. I turn and lean against the side of the car, focusing on an ancient Miller Beer clock mounted on the wall.

My father puts down his tools and wipes off his hands, leaning against the side of the car next to me. "It sounds like she doesn't have much of a choice, though."

I pause. How do I explain what Carlisle told me? I'm not sure I fully understand it myself. And I'm... conflicted... about everything.

"She's not sure if she's going to have the surgery," I say. "What?"

"She doesn't want to be... paralyzed... disabled. It's the most probable outcome for the surgery."

"That's terrible but the only alternative is... "

He stops talking and I can feel him turn to look at me. I swallow hard, suddenly unable to breathe even though my heart is fluttering like a hummingbird.

"Oh Matty," he says, using the nickname he abandoned when he gave me the speech about wet dreams and how to behave with real girls. The anguish in his voice tells me that he understands everything. His arm is a heavy weight across my shoulders and I appreciate the grounding it gives me when it feels like I'm going to fly apart.

"She's been planning to kill herself since before we even met. She doesn't want to live if it involves crutches or a wheelchair or anything like that." I turn to face him, hoping that I see some kind of answer in his gaze. "And this feels like it's Mari all over again. Karma, God, the fucking universe paying me back for not being there for her. For failing her."

He moves quickly, big hands around the back of my neck, forcing me to maintain eye contact.

"The God I know isn't going to dish out payback. Never." He is vehement, fierce in his tone even though his grip is gentle. "And you did not fail Mari. She made her choice and we all had to live with it because it was her decision to make. She didn't make it lightly or without considering all of us but she couldn't deny what she wanted, what she needed, just to live for us. I didn't like it then and I hate it now but I can't fault her for the choice she made."

I push him away, anger rising and eclipsing the hurt and the fear.

"How can you say that Dad? She gave up! She didn't fight!"

"If you think for one minute that your sister didn't fight then you weren't paying attention. She fought and got the chemo and puked her guts out for weeks. She lost weight and cried when her hair fell out and endured something no parent should ever have to watch their kid go through." He raises a fist, white knuckled and shaking and places it over his heart, his expression open and broken. I want to look away but I can't. "And when they gave her the options, she chose to go out on her terms. She knew she was giving up time but she wanted what time she had to be different. I didn't want her to make that choice but I understand that it was hers to make." He steps forward, lowering his voice and placing his hand on my shoulder. "And no matter how you or I feel about it, Carlisle will make her own choice and you will either be able to support her or not. *That* will be your choice."

I know he's right. Mari was right. Carlisle will be right with whatever she chooses to do. I just don't know what I can do.

"I failed Mari. I don't want to do the same with Carlisle," I whisper.

"I know you think you let your sister down, the family down, and all I can tell you is that none of us think you did. If Mari did, she never said one word about it."

I pace away from him and throw out there the one thing that has never been said between us. I can't even look at him.

"I wasn't there to say goodbye. I was drunk and fucking some girl whose name I still can't remember."

He closes his eyes and his fists grip at his side as he lets out a long, slow breath. When he makes eye contact with me I see disappointment in their depths but overwhelmingly I just see pity and love and something splits open deep inside me. I grab my abdomen, convinced that if I look down, I will see my guts and lifeblood spilling out and onto my feet.

"Zane never told me where he found you but I thought it was something like that."

I nod, bracing myself for what I have coming, what I deserve. "Don't you hate me? Hate my failure?"

"I could never hate you but I am disappointed in you," he says, honestly but with no heat. "But I know you've hated yourself for it enough for the whole world's judgment and I think you need to stop. Mari didn't hate you. She said there was nothing left unsaid between the two of you and she was at peace about it."

"I wish I'd been there," I say, choking on the bitterness of the truth. "Wish I'd had the guts to say goodbye."

"And that is something you'll have to put at rest for yourself. Give it time and you'll work it out," Dad says as he leans against the car, watching me closely. "All we can do is take what happened and try to make it into something that helps, that heals. Maybe that's medical school for you. Maybe it's loving Carlisle. I don't know."

"I don't know if I love Carlisle," I say, the words rough on my tongue. They taste of a bitter half-truth. I know how I feel about her—I just don't know if I can let myself follow everything that goes with it.

My dad shifts a look at me that says he doesn't believe what I just said but he lets it pass, instead saying, "I don't know if she's made up her mind or not but you've got to make up your mind to either be all in or all out. Whether she decides to go out on her own terms or spend the rest of her life in a wheelchair, if you don't love her enough to stand by her through all of it, then get out of the way so that she can find the man who will."

It isn't the answer I was hoping he'd give me, the solution to all my problems, but it's a direction. Something for me to consider along with everything else we talked about tonight.

I walk out of the garage, waving my mom off as I head to my car and climb inside. I pull out onto the road and make turn after turn, sticking to the two and one lane roads headed deeper into the country. The sun slides across the sky as I drive, stopping only to fill up the tank and grab a bottle of water. My phone is buzzing in the seat beside me but I ignore it. Zane. My mom. Zane again.

I need to figure out what I'm going to do.

One part of me wants to give in to the rage and crash this vehicle into the nearest tree, as if me giving up my life will somehow give Carlisle's back to her. The ultimate penance for being a shitty brother and a coward.

Can I learn from what I did wrong before and get it right this time? Can I be the man Carlisle will need? Can I be the man who will watch her struggle with whoever she'll be after the surgery? Can I be the man who will hold her hand as she passes on her own terms?

Can I actually give her up?

The lights in Nashville shine like costume jewelry on a pretty girl when I head back into the city with the top down and the wind drowning out everything but my thoughts. My head is spinning, my heart catching with each thought of Carlisle, each memory.

I cannot get past the moment in my bed. Not the sex, not the way she controls me with a brush across my skin or the press of her lips on mine but the slide of our hands together. Fingers entwined in the perfect weave, stronger together than apart. The way she tightened her grip on mine when I whispered "*Tesoro*".

My treasure.

The one I was not looking for but found buried under the shit of all of our issues, our pasts, our pain. Carlisle shines like gold, warming me from the inside out. Repairing the broken bits and bringing the others back to life. *Mi Tesoro.*

I pull in to one of the empty spots on the street in front of her apartment, weighing what I'm going to say to her but knowing that it has to be tonight. It has to be right now. I look up and see the lights on in her living room and I take the stairs at a run, bypassing the elevator and power pulling off the railing to help me get there faster. I run down the hallway, banging on the door as soon as I get it within arm's reach.

I keep knocking even when I hear steps approaching and the murmurings from within that "they are coming as fast as they can". I hold my breath as the door swings open and I face an older woman with Carlisle's red-gold hair and freckles on her nose. Close behind her is a man whose intense stare I've seen leveled at me many times when his daughter is trying to figure me out. Carlisle is a fair blend of them both, stealing the best parts to mix into her own unique beauty.

Behind them both, Carlisle steps forward, her hair pulled up in a ponytail and she's wearing no make-up. She looks pale, the red around her eyes betraying her if she's trying to keep her tears a secret. I want to take her face in my hands, wipe every single one, and kiss her until she forgets her reasons to cry. Just for a little while.

"Mateo." Her father knows my name so I'm guessing that their daughter has brought them up to speed on the man she's been sleeping with. His face is rigid and I can tell by the way he's holding his hands at his side that he's itching to throw me out. "This isn't a good time."

I shake my head. "I think it's the perfect time for me to tell you that I love your daughter." Carlisle gasps and I turn to her, taking the several steps it takes for me to cover the distance to stand right in front of her. "I love you and I'm here. No matter what you decide to do I will stay with you, but I'm hoping you choose to stay with me because I love you. So much."

She reaches for me and I pull her into my arms, exhaling when she burrows in close and hangs on tight.

"I love you too," she whispers.

It's all the answer I need for right now.

Chapter Seventeen

Carlisle

"Do you two have enough towels, Mom?" I ask.

I look around the second bedroom in my apartment, making sure my parents have what they need. Tomorrow is my surgery and after a week of test, more tests, and invasively personal questions, I have the green light to jump off a cliff into the vast unknown.

That isn't entirely true.

I know these things: my chances of dying on the table are miniscule; my chances of using some form of crutches or a wheelchair for the rest of my life is at ninety percent. If there is a ten percent miracle out there for me, I might walk forever unaided but I have a sneaky suspicion that I used that miracle on surviving the bomb blast in the first place. I've heard over and over this week that I am a very lucky girl.

And this week I believe them.

Because Mateo is in the other room waiting for me.

My mom turns to look at me from her place at the desk and she's got "the face" on. Now I know why my dad is out on the balcony. He's not watching the city lights, he's avoiding the big emotional after-school special moment my mom clearly wants to have. I take two steps towards the door and she crooks her finger at me in the "come here" gesture and then points to the end of the bed.

I sit my ass down because what else am I supposed to do. Her baby is going under the knife tomorrow and she wants to say whatever it is she needs to say. I guess I should say some things too.

We are not an extraordinarily emotive family. My dad is a stoic rancher, fifth generation and a Texan to the core. Mom is an Alabama beauty who went to the University of Texas to get her teaching degree and ended up living on a ranch and raising two kids. Andrew, is a big, bad Marine and loves it. You hug him at your own risk.

"Emma Carlisle," she says, using my seldom-used first name. "I am so grateful you are having the surgery. I know you're bearing the burden for all of us. The physical therapy, the uncertain future. We love you for it."

I shake my head. She's got it wrong.

"Mom, I'm not doing it for you... "

She cuts me off with a wave of her hand. "For Mateo then. I don't care who it's for I just... " And then she starts to cry and I sit there feeling like a total asshole for making my mom cry. "You have no idea what it's like to watch someone you love die so young and so full of promise."

I gasp and she stutters a bit, her hands waving in front of her face like she's trying to suck the words back in. I know she didn't mean them the way they came out. I throw out all my usual hang-ups and rush to comfort her and gather her close in a hug. If there was ever at time for the Queens to get huggy, this is probably it.

"It's okay mom. I know you didn't mean Aaron." I rub her back as she cries on my shoulder and I remain strong, bearing her pain and letting her find her peace as I can. In an ideal world, she should be the one holding me as I weep and wail but I'm not built that way. I might look like my mom but I'm my daddy's girl where it counts. I can be strong for her and anyone who needs me to be. I've seen me do it. "It's okay. I'm going to be fine. Dr. Bertrand says so."

I hold her for a while longer, giving her time to pull herself together as I correct her assumption.

"I'm not doing this for you, or dad, or Mateo. I'm doing it for me."

She pulls away and looks at me, her eyes narrow with disbelief. "You told me you were planning on *killing* yourself. The only thing that changed since then is Mateo Butler arriving on the scene and while I'm beyond grateful, I do think it's a little fast."

Wait. What?

"What are you talking about mom?" I release her and scoot back on the bed not sure where this made such a weird turn.

"It's just that we've never heard about him and we get here and he comes running and declares his love and suddenly you're having the surgery. I just think it's a little soon for you to count on this working out between the two of you."

"Nice way to tell me you don't like my boyfriend, mom."

"It's not that I don't like him. He's wonderful, handsome and he can't keep his eyes off you. But what you're getting ready to do, all the hard work and the uncertainty would take its toll on a couple who had been together for years." She reaches out and grabs my hand, giving me a smile that tells me she's not trying to freak me out just hours before major surgery. "The kind of bond you need to get through this type of life-change takes time and you guys just haven't had that time."

I nod, completely understanding what she just said. She's not wrong. But Mateo and I aren't guaranteed to work even if we had been together twenty years. Nobody is.

"I get it mom. All I can tell you is that I love him and he loves me and we're going to ride this out together. Whatever happens will happen but I think we've got what it takes." I squeeze her hand and stand to go back to my room. "But I'm not doing this for Mateo. I am doing this because of how he makes me feel." She's obviously confused so I try my best to explain it better. "I loved Aaron and losing him killed off my ability to hope but Mateo gave it back to me. And as Dr. Shrieve reminded me hope is not a guarantee of the future but it's a reason to stick around. So I decided to stick and around see what life has in store for me. I hope it is with Mateo, I plan on it, but I know better than anyone that the best laid plans can be gone in the blink of an eye."

"I think I get that," she says as she rises and comes over to give me one more kiss. "But whatever the reason, I'm so glad you decided to do this. Your father and I will do whatever it is you need us to do. We love you Emma Carlisle."

"I know mom and I love you too."

I leave her room and pad silently across the living room where Livvy is crashed out on the sofa. I told her she didn't need to come but there was no stopping her and I'm so glad she came. She's the sister of my heart and since Andrew couldn't get leave to come home, she can help Mateo handle my parents. Dr. Bertrand already looks like he wants to run when my mom is around.

I slip into my room and hear the shower running in my bathroom. I kick off my flip flops, peel off my capri's, and sit on the edge of the bed in just a t-shirt and my underwear. I should probably try to go to sleep, take one of the pills Dr. Bertrand gave me and float off into oblivion. But I don't want to do that. Not tonight. I have plans.

The shower stops running and I listen as Mateo pulls a towel off the rack and closes the door. I close my eyes and try to track the sounds he makes as he completes the most mundane of tasks. Brushing his teeth. Opening the cabinet door and using his deodorant and then closing the door again. No shave tonight. He'll save it for tomorrow morning.

He's been here with me for the past week and we've quickly adopted our domestic routine. I will miss this nightly ritual, waiting for him to come to the bed we share together. I love sleeping with his big frame wrapped around me, the hair on his chest and legs tickling my skin, the soft puff of his even breaths on my neck, the possessive hand he splays across my belly. Tomorrow night I will stay in the hospital for the first of several nights and then they will move me a long-term rehabilitation facility affiliated with Vanderbilt University.

I'm keeping my apartment but I have no idea when I'll be back. I just can't give it up. It would seem too ... permanent.

Mateo emerges from the bathroom, the residual steam following him out as he fully opens the door. His dark hair is wet, one of my big, fluffy towels wrapped around his waist.

He sees me and he smiles. That bright, gut-punching smile that makes me glad I'm sitting down because it reduces me to goo every single time.

He is so hot. His muscles. The washboard abs and those cut lines angling down like arrows pointing to the good stuff. His large hands that can do hard labor at his cousin's house and then touch me so gently that I fall apart like a broken window night after night.

But I don't want gentle tonight. I need to feel him.

"Hey," he says walking towards me and stopping just in front of where I sit. He looks down, tiny droplets of water trailing down his chest and just begging for me to lick them off. His lips twist in a carnal grin when he guesses what I'm thinking.

"How are your parents?" He asks.

He wants to talk about my mom and dad? I look at him more closely and I see the laughter twitching at the corner of his mouth. He's teasing me.

I reach out and grab the edge of the towel and tug, dropping it to the floor. He's only half hard but I know I can fix that.

"I don't want to talk about my parents or the surgery or any other fucking thing right now. All I want to do is have you fuck me so that for one last night I can feel like myself. A memory to last for a lifetime. Can you do that for me?"

He's starting down at me, all traces of humor gone from his face now and his dick is getting harder as the second pass. He licks his lips but his voice is still hoarse when he speaks. "I can do that for you."

"Good." I nod and swallow, thinking about what I crave most. "I want to suck you off first. Make me."

His eyes flare at my demand, his pupils now blown so that he looks like he's on something. I know he's only high on me and that turns me on even more. I feel powerful as my hand circles his cock, loving the feel of the hard length as it slides over my palm. Mateo grabs my hand and lowers it to my side, pressing it down on the bed.

"Keep your hands to yourself," he demands while taking my head in between his big hands and holding me still while he rubs my mouth with his dick.

We stare at each other, something primal and achingly sensual suspended between us. I feel dirty and powerful in all the best ways and I moan when he rolls his hips and his cock presses against my lips. I lick them and open as he presses inside with his hard, hot thickness. The thick flare of his cockhead glides over my tongue leaving behind a salty, sexy taste of pre-come.

I open wider, looking forward to the ache I will have in my jaw tomorrow, and Mateo sets a rhythm. He's not gentle, sensing my mood and riding it out as he fucks my mouth and takes me out of my head and all the scary places its been lately. He pulls halfway out and then sinks back in again, bumping the back of my throat when I reach up and cup his ass, digging my fingers into the taut muscle there. My head starts to swim as he starts talking.

"Fuck Carlisle, that's so good baby. You're so wet and hot." He groans, his grip on my head tighter as his thrusts get faster. He's using me just like I want, the only thing I feel is the way my body responds to his, the wetness between my thighs and the ache in my breasts. I feel alive. Whole. Feminine.

"I'm close. If you don't want it down your throat let me know."

I don't. I want him inside me when he explodes. I pull off him and use my grip on his ass to maneuver him around and push him down on the bed. He lands with a bouncing thud and we both huff out a quick laugh of surprise. Mateo and Carlisle. Still laughing when we make love. I hope that part never ends.

I reach over to my side table and get a condom out of the drawer. I open the packet and crawl over him and roll it down his length, loving the way his body bucks up when I give I few leisurely strokes.

"How do you want me baby?" He asks, lying in a

submissive pose on the bed. "I'm yours however you want me. All I want to do is make you feel good. As many times as you want."

I run through the many ways I can have him take me. Mateo is an amazing lover and I'll come, over and over as he promises if I want. But tonight I want to be in charge, I need to have that control over our pleasure.

"Just like that. Hands on the headboard." He sucks in a breath but does as I direct him and moves around until his head is on the pillows, long body spread out. I lick my lips when he raises his arms and grips the wrought iron bars on my headboard.

I straddle him, resting my wet pussy against the hard length of him, undulating my hips just enough to cause sparks behind my eyelids and see his grip on the bars tighten. I trail my fingertips down his chest, tracing the cut of his abs, rubbing the hard pebbles of his nipples. His thighs are shaking, his feet digging into the mattress.

"I'm going to ride you, Mateo. Don't move until I tell you to."

He nods, jaw tight with his effort to remain still.

I position my body over his hard erection and I slide down, the glide so easy with how wet I am. Nobody gets me off like Mateo. Nobody. I suck in a huge breath as he fills me, stretching me, the first few moments walking that pleasure /pain path I love so much. I memorize all of it, committing it to memory and hoping this isn't the last time I feel this way.

I don't want to be in this alone so I keep my gaze on him. I could get drunk on the play of emotions across his face as I begin a slow up and down ride on his dick. I take my time, enjoying the moments as they pass by with us joined, suspended in our pleasure... together.

"You like that?" I ask and he nods, his grip making the muscle in his forearm go taut. "Do you want me to go faster?"

"I love being buried in your pussy. Fast, slow. I just want to stay inside you forever," he confesses. The naked honesty on his face making my chest hurt with just how loved I know

I am.

I lean forward, placing my breasts at mouth level and whisper, "Suck on them."

Mateo lifts his head, capturing my right nipple in his mouth and he sucks on it hard and long. The pulse of lightening from his touch races across my belly and settles in my clit as it rubs against his abdominal muscles with each of my strokes. I let my ride speed up as he licks and sucks and lightly bites my nipples until they are sensitive to his every caress. I can feel the beginning of my orgasm low in my belly.

"Fuck me Mateo," I growl in his ear and it sets him free to move.

He bucks his hips up as I piston mine down and our bodies meet in a frantic press of hard cock and soft pussy. His hand remains on the headboard but I don't need them on me. I just need him inside me, filling me.

I want it to last longer but he returns his mouth to my breast and takes a nipple in his mouth and begins a fast flicker of his tongue against it. I explode. On him. All over him. My orgasm bows my back and forces me to lose my rhythm.

Mateo lets go of the headboard and grabs my hips, forcing me to follow his pace until he stiffens underneath me and yells with the force of his release.

We probably disturbed the neighbors or woke my parents but I don't care. I needed this. What could be my last time to feel this way, to feel this, period.

I send up a silent prayer that this part of me will remain. That this next step will not strip me of what to me is so essential to my femininity, my enjoyment of life. I feel ashamed at my thoughts, knowing I should be grateful to be alive, to have this opportunity to reduce my pain and possible improve my mobility.

Sex should be the least of my worries but with this young, virile man panting under me, I wonder how I will make him happy. Will he ever look at me with his blue eyes filled with desire and want?

I knew all of this would hit me sometime.

I collapse against him as my emotions bowl me over like a freight train. I don't even realize I'm crying until Mateo pulls me in close and starts making those soothing noises against my ear. I cling to him, letting him tell me that everything is going to be fine.

That he's got me.

That we are in this together.

I listen to his words.

My lover's lullaby makes it bearable until I crash into a deep, dreamless sleep.

Chapter Eighteen

Carlisle

My mouth tastes like a wet swimsuit I left in my gym bag for two days, and people are talking about me.

I try to crack my eyes open, fighting the pull of whatever they have in my system to drag me back into oblivion. But this room is bright, I'm tired of sleeping, and I've got to stop my mom from telling everyone the story about how my swimsuit strap broke at one of my first competitions and I flashed the entire crowd when I pulled myself out of the pool and jumped around in victory.

I swallow a couple of times, my first attempt at speech producing nothing. I swallow some more and lift my hand in an attempt to make a gesture that will communicate "shut the hell up" most effectively. It works because the story stops and I hear chairs scraping and people gasping all around my bed.

"Carlisle," my mother is on my left, her voice loud in my ear. "Hold on baby, we're calling the nurse."

Fuck the nurse. I want a drink of water.

I crack my eyes open enough to see the pitcher of water sitting on my bedside table and I point to it, clearing my throat.

My dad figures it out first and reaches for the pitcher and shakes out ice cubes into a cup with a spoon and hands it off to my mom. She scoops some up and feeds it to me and I sigh in ecstasy. Best ice cubes in the whole world. She spoons me another and I open my eyes, looking for Mateo.

He's there, on my right side, looking tired and stressed but also relieved and like he still loves me. He didn't change his mind about all this craziness and run for the hills while Dr. Bertrand was digging around in my back. Thank God.

"Hi," I croak out at him. I tell myself that I sound sexy but in truth it's more like I have a six-pack-a-day smoking habit. His smile and his hand closing over mine makes me not give a shit anymore.

"Hi." He puts my hand to his lips and presses a soft kiss against my knuckles and my heart does this jumpy thing that makes the monitor's bleepy sounds speed up and my parents start laughing as he leans over and kisses me gently. "*Tesoro.*"

"How do you feel baby?" my mom asks.

"We called for the doctor," my dad says, sneaking his large hand around my mom to squeeze my shoulder. "How do you feel?"

And that is the question, isn't it?

I begin to concentrate on my body under the covers, trying to detect anything from my waist down. I'm not sure what I'm supposed to be looking for at this point. It was fully explained to me that the meds for post-op pain might mask much of the sensation for a while.

"Yes, Carlisle, how do you feel?" Dr. Bertrand asks as he walks into the room, a nurse following close behind. My parents move away from my bedside, allowing the professionals access to the equipment and the patient. I can tell by the look on his face that he's seconds away from telling them all to leave and I feel panic building in my gut.

When Teo tries to pull back I grip his hand tightly and look at him. "Stay with me."

"Always," he answers, squeezing my fingers lightly before looking up at the doctor. "Don't make me break my promise, Doc."

Doctor Bertrand frowns, clearly displeased with not having me all to himself. He looks at Mateo and then at my parents and he relents.

"I can tell that I will lose whatever argument I try to start so I'll just cry uncle now." He taps on his tablet and pulls up what I can only presume is my record and reads for a few seconds before placing it on the side table and pulling a pen light out of his pocket. He shines it in my eyes. "Any nausea?

Vertigo? Blurry vision?"

"No."

He looks at me, his gaze assessing for a few seconds before he grabs the edge of my blanket and pulls it down, exposing my lower body in the hideous hospital gown. From the slightly elevated position of my head and shoulders, I can see the bolster under my knees and I mentally tell my legs to flex against the cushion.

Nothing.

Doctor Bertrand glances up at me, clearly trying to gauge my reaction. "Carlisle, as I told your family, the surgery went very well. There was more shrapnel than anticipated and the scar tissue from your prior surgeries made removal difficult but we got it all." He pulls an instrument out of his pocket, a metal rod the size of a pen with a rounded tip on one end and a pointy tip on the other. "There will be significant swelling for at least a week and we will treat it with anti-inflammatories. The pain will be managed by narcotics for a couple of days but then we will switch you to higher dosages of non-narcotic medication. We don't want the drugs to inhibit your participation in your physical therapy."

I nod at this and he stares at me for two beats before moving to my feet. He lowers the instrument and uses it to press against the sole of my foot.

"Can you feel that?"

I shake my head. "No."

He moves his position and I can see his hands flex as he presses the instrument forward. I squeeze Teo's hand, willing myself to feel something. I close my eyes, searching for the sensation. Nothing. I open my eyes and shake my head. "No. Nothing."

I glance towards my parents and they both are as white as the bleach-scented sheets on my bed. My dad's arms are wrapped around my mom and I can see, even at this distance, that they are trembling. I'm glad I'm not the only one freaking out. I'm also glad I have Teo who is steady as rock next me, not even a flicker of worry across his face. I take his courage and inhale it, letting it soak into my body and calm me.

Dr. Bertrand places his hands, palms flat against the bottoms of my feet and looks at me, his expression determined and encouraging. It's as if he's willing me to pass this next test, as if it is the most important.

I ignore the icy tendril of fear chasing along my skin and the cold sweat that chills me in the cool hospital air. I hold my breath, waiting for his instructions.

"Press against my hands, as hard as you can."

I look down at my feet and I shiver because right now they feel like they belong to someone else. Or they are those fake feet that peek out from the end of the box in the magician's act when he tries to convince you that he's really sawing that chick in half.

"Carlisle. You can do it," he says, giving me an encouraging nod that reminds me of my swim coach. Sometimes only his gruff voice and that curt nod could get my ass off the starting block. Now, I'm standing on this new starting block and I have no idea if I will shoot through the water or sink like a stone. I almost wish I could stay in this moment and never know the answer but I never have been and I never will be that big of a coward.

I close my eyes and I concentrate, squeezing Teo's hand even tighter as I order my limbs to obey the command from my brain. The seconds seem to drag on forever and I feel tears welling up in my eyes as nothing happens. It's like the time I woke up in the hospital in Europe after the bombing and nothing worked the right way and the love of my life was dead.

"Okay, relax a minute," Dr. Bertrand says, removing his hands from the bottom of my feet.

"Let me try again," I blurt out, panic making my voice shake and quaver and giving away the fact that I'm on the verge of tears. "I can do this. Let me try again."

He flicks a glance at my parents and Mateo and then returns his focus back to me. He leans forward on my bed, placing his hands flat on the mattress on each side of my legs.

When he speaks, it is the same calm, level tone he's had since my first meeting with him. No nonsense. Practical. Infuriatingly honest.

"I had two criteria for taking your case, Carlisle. The first was physical, the extent of damage to your nervous system and the likelihood that surgery would help you maintain the most mobility." He pauses, his eyes never leaving my own. "The second criteria was patient attitude and I believe is the most important of all. To get through all of the hard work that is coming your way, you need to be a hard worker who is also a fighter. Someone who doesn't let one small failure keep you from working until you achieve what you want. I knew that the young woman who endured years of grueling training and then won twelve gold medals had the attitude I was looking for. I knew you would fight and not let one little failure today stop you from getting up and doing it again tomorrow." He straightens, moving his hands back to the soles of my feet and keeps speaking. "So, I want you to try again and even if you don't succeed I know you'll try again tomorrow."

He nods and I blink back the emotion blurring my vision and take a deep breath. I'm shaking, scared to death, but I'm not ready to let go of the girl he was talking about. Once I made the decision to have this surgery, my course was set and now it is no different than making it to the summer games. No matter what, I'll be back tomorrow.

I concentrate. I squeeze Mateo's hand. I push.

Seconds pass by and nothing happens and then I feel it. It isn't much and his hands only move back a tiny amount but they move. I blink. Mateo yells. My mother cries.

Doctor Bertrand smiles.

I lean back on my pillows, exhausted from just that tiny bit of effort. My dad leans over and kisses my cheek and I kiss him back, loving the familiar rumble of his voice in my ear. "Love you baby. So proud of you."

Doctor Bertrand, embracing his role as chief buzz killer, holds his hands up and stops the party that has erupted in my room.

"That's excellent. I cannot predict how much mobility you will have in the end but that is a very good sign. You have months of hard work ahead of you. I know you can do it." He looks around the room at my parents and Mateo and his face sobers a bit. "Like we discussed in our pre-operative meetings, you need to figure out your schedules. Carlisle will need your help but you need to take care of yourselves, get out of here when she is in therapy, sleep in a real bed." He gives Mateo a meaningful glance, "Attend classes."

"Thank you Doctor Bertrand," I force out, quickly feeling all of the emotions crashing down on me. I don't know whether I want to cry or scream or laugh. I just know that I don't want do it with all these people in the room. I tug Mateo down to me and I hide my face in his shoulder, biting back the tears that I now know are coming. He sits down on the bed beside me and holds me as close as all the tubes, wires and my current condition will allow. He smells like coffee, sunshine, and Mateo and I drink him in and try to steal his strength.

"Doctor, let's talk out in the hallway," my mom says on the other side of the bed and I am grateful when she ushers everyone out of my room.

The silence isn't empty for long before I fill it with the sobs I can't hold back. Mateo holds me, silent but solid as I ugly cry all over his t-shirt. He doesn't try to get me to stop, doesn't tell me it will be all right. He just holds me. Lets me lose my shit with as much dignity as possible while sitting here in a gown with my ass hanging out of it and my hair in a walk-of-shame-without-the-fun-orgasm mess on the top of my head.

"That scared me," I admit, brushing some of the wetness off my cheeks as I feel the worst of it pass. "It was like the first time... when I woke up."

"I think that's a normal reaction, to remember that time." Mateo kisses the top of my head and squeezes me tighter. He pulls back and I'm surprised at the tracks of moisture on his cheeks. I raise an eyebrow and trace one of the tears. He shrugs. "I'm not even handing over my man card because even Chuck Norris would cry over the shit that just went down here."

"Oh really? You invoke the name of the great Chuck? I don't know... " I laugh at the death glare he gives me and tug him down to me so I can give him a kiss. It's a light one, tender and I hope he can feel all the gratitude I have for him in the touch. I decide not to take the chance and just tell him. "Thank you Teo. Thank you for being here, for loving me."

He smiles and brushes my hair back from my face, his warmth keeping away the chill of the room. "Loving you is the easiest thing... like breathing. No matter what, we'll do this together."

I snuggle against him, enjoying the moment and brushing aside any doubt or fear about what is to come. My mom's worries edge in but I push them away and focus on what I know: I'm going to beat this, and Mateo and I have what it takes to make it.

Chapter Nineteen

Mateo

"Mr. Butler can I see you after class?"

I stop as I gather my things to leave the lab, turning to face my instructor, Dr. Steinberg. He doesn't look happy— he never looks happy—but the alarming part of his current look is that it is aimed at me. He is a hardass and he's been waiting to chew on mine since day one. My lab partners all give me pity glances but they aren't waiting around to be sucked into the vortex of fury that swirls around him.

"See you at group study later?" Adam asks as he slings his messenger bag across his body.

"Yeah. At your place?"

"Yep. See you later." He sneaks a peek at Steinberg and then runs away like the flying monkeys are after him.

"Mr. Butler, I'm afraid we must have an unpleasant conversation."

I sigh and put down my backpack, realizing this will not be a quick conversation. I sneak a look at my watch but I'm not sneaky enough because when I look back at him, he's glaring with renewed fire.

"Am I making you late for something?"

"My girlfriend is recovering from spinal surgery and she's in rehab and I haven't seen her all day... " I let my sentence trail off when I realize that he is uninterested.

"Maybe that explains your lack of focus and your poor attendance at lecture and group labs. I understand you slept through a lecture earlier this week and it's becoming a common occurrence."

"I know I've been preoccupied. I've got a lot to juggle right now but I'll figure it out," I answer, feeling the hot creep of embarrassment crawl up my neck. "I just need a little time."

"This course lasts three months. You have lecture and lab every day, five days per week. This was all in your materials."

"I know, Dr. Steinberg... "

"Mr. Butler you are exceptionally bright and you grasp even the most complex concepts quickly and thoroughly... " I think about thanking him but even I can hear the "but" coming. "... but that is only when you are here and actually present. I need to warn you that you are in danger of failing this course but as we are only three weeks in, you have time to turn your behavior around."

I'm stunned by his words. I know I've missed a few things and failed a couple of quizzes but I thought I could pull it out in the end. I always have before. It's just been a son-of-a-bitch to juggle school and Carlisle. She needs me and it's hard to focus on this place when she's battling it out on the other side of town.

I find my tongue and say the only thing I can say. "I'll fix it Dr. Steinberg. You have my word."

"I hope you will Mr. Butler. I think you have a bright future in this profession if you can focus on what needs to be done."

He hands me an envelope and walks away like he hasn't thrown a firebomb into the middle of my life. I open the envelope and pull out the paper, unfolding it and noting the medical school letterhead. I skim it, noting that it gives the same dire warning I just received in person. I refold it and shove it into my backpack. I'll deal with it later, right now I'll miss seeing Carlisle at all today if I don't get moving now.

I drive across town, irritated by the evening traffic but too distracted by my warning from Dr. Steinberg to really get worked up. I think about how I need to adjust my schedule and all of it adds up to seeing less of Carlisle. And that is the last thing I want to do.

She's wheelchair bound for now but they are working on moving her up to crutches in the near future. The therapy is grueling, physically exhausting and she is in a great deal of pain most of the time because she doesn't want to take the really good drugs because they make her loopy. So, she toughs it out, grinds her teeth and rolls around with dark circles under her eyes because she's not sleeping well. Her mom told me that she was the same when she was training, nothing was going to stop her except injury or collapse. She's that driven.

I want to be with her. I need to be with her. I promised her that I would be there and I refuse to break my promise. She is my world, more than this course, and that is the crux of my problem. It isn't the first time I've wondered if medical school is where I need to be right now.

I pull into the parking lot of the high-end rehabilitation facility where Carlisle will be living for at least the next nine months. She's lucky to have a single room and the place goes out of its way to not look like a hospital but I can tell she's already itching to leave and live independently.

I want her to move in with me when she gets out although I haven't brought it up yet. Her parents still give me the side-eye and I've overheard a couple of conversations between them that begin and end with "this has happened way too fast".

I jump out of my car, grabbing my backpack as I leave, hoping I can sneak in some study time before group tonight. The staff just wave me on as I enter, smiling as I practically run past. They love Carlisle and the rest of her entourage are included in the glow.

I knock and, hearing nothing, enter her room, throwing my bag on the loveseat under the window that overlooks the flower garden in the interior courtyard. Carlisle can afford a nice place and this one goes out of its way to not look like a hospital. She has a hospital type bed but the floors are warm oak laminate and there is real wood furniture instead of the melamine and pressboard stuff you usually see. Her mother brought in some of her artwork, a few blankets and her books from her apartment and the effect is cozy. As Carlisle says, "It's not home but it will do in a pinch."

No one is in here and I check my watch again. She should be done with her afternoon session and getting ready for dinner. The sound of the shower is faint through the closed door but I walk over and tap lightly. I get no response so I push the door open and I'm met with a wave of steam from the hot water running.

The first thing I see is Carlisle's wheelchair pulled up close to the rimless shower next to the location of the shower seat she needs to use.

The second thing I see is Carlisle. On the shower bench. Crying.

I am at her side in two steps, not caring that the shower spray is soaking me from head to toe.

"Carlisle, baby." I check her over, trying to see if she is hurt, if there is anything I can do. "What's wrong? Do you want me to call a nurse?"

She's crying so hard that I debate waiting for her reply. "Carlisle, you're scaring me. Are you hurt? Do I need... "

"It hurts all the time," she stammers out, her hands clutching the edge of the shower stall in a white-knuckle grip. She reaches out one hand to dig her fingers into her calf, pressing hard into the muscle. "It hurts all the fucking time but I can't feel anything! I work and I work. I practically kill myself to get out of that chair but nothing... " She breaks down in a deeper sob as she rakes her nails over her skin, raising angry red marks. "... nothing changes."

Aw fuck. My heart breaks. Shatters into a million pieces in my chest and I bite back the urge to rail against all the shit she has to bear. But she doesn't need me to scream alongside her, she needs me to be the wall of stone she can batter herself against. Her safe place.

"Hey, hey." I reach up to turn off the water and snag a towel from the peg nearby and wrap it around her shoulders. She's shivering a little in the air conditioning and I also feel the chill as my wet clothes stick to my body. I brush aside the discomfort and pat her down as she really begins to shiver. "It's okay. Let's get you warm and you can tell me about what happened."

Whatever fight she had went down the drain with water and she collapses against me and I hold her tight, willing my body heat into her. If I could give her the use of my legs, I would. I know she's frustrated at the pace of her recovery and this might be the culmination of days of frustration or it might be the result of a major setback.

Either way, I'll be here for her.

I stand, careful of the wet floor as I get to my feet and I scoop her up in my arms. My memory immediately flashes back to the first time I did this for her, the day I think of as the time we really began. That day, when she trusted me with her weakness, was the beginning of this journey together.

I walk into her room trying to rub warmth into her skin and to soothe her when one of the night nurses, Susan, steps into the room. She takes one look at the two of us, soaking wet and shivering, and she rushes to my side.

"Did she have an accident in the shower?" I can feel her hands touching Carlisle, checking for any injury. "Where did you find her?"

"I'm fine," Carlisle says from where her head is lying on my shoulder. "I didn't fall."

"I found her in there seated on the bench. She was… " I consider what I will tell her when I feel Carlisle's fingers squeeze my arm. In spite of all she's been through, she's sensitive to anyone seeing her cry or anything less than the girl standing on the top of the tier with a medal around her neck. "She was upset."

Susan locks eyes with me over Carlisle's shoulder and nods, her eyes full of understanding. "I'll get more towels and I'll grab you some scrubs and throw your wet clothes in the dryer."

She leaves and I peel Carlisle off me enough to see her face. Her eyes are red, mascara smeared and her nose a bright pink. Her hair is starting to curl in those loose waves I love but her lips are tinged with blue. Susan returns with the towels and places a double layer on the bed so that I can sit Carlisle down and do what she needs me to do.

She is quiet while I help her dry off, taking over when I get to her hair and even accepting the comb when I snag it off her vanity.

"Do you want the Captain America pajamas or the ones Livvy sent you?" I hold up the sleep t-shirt that says "I've got 99 problems and liking men isn't one of them" for her inspection. "I vote for this one because it makes all the staff feel sorry for me since I have no chance with you at all."

She laughs a little at my joke and reaches out for it. "Yes, that one."

I bring it to her and she lifts her arms up, inviting me to slide it over her head. The move is sexy and I lean over to lightly kiss her, whispering against her mouth. "Have I told you how much I love that you hate underwear?"

I realize about two seconds too late that I've said the wrong thing when she pulls back from me and turns away. I'm not bothered by the fact that sex is off the table for recovery reasons, it's her refusal to talk to me about it at all. She can discuss any aspect of her recovery with me but she shuts me out whenever the topic of a future sex life comes up with her doctors if I'm around. I know that a sacral level spinal injury can cause issues with sexuality but I have no idea what's going on with her.

Sex is the least of our issues but it's one of the many that have created the tiniest gap between us. It's nothing we can't fix and I guess it's understandable but I hate it all the same. I just wish she would talk to me.

"Thank you, Teo," she says as I help her move her legs and slide under the covers.

"Hey, anything for you," I say, positioning her pillow behind her in the spot she likes it best. I perch on the side of the bed and lean down to kiss her temple, murmuring against her hair. "You want to tell me what happened?"

She pauses for the briefest second and I will her to answer me but she shakes her head in the end. "Not right now. I think I need to sleep for a bit."

I bite back my sigh and pull away to look into her eyes. Emerald green with flecks of gold look up at me and while I know she's holding back, I don't see anything that gives me a clue about what is going on.

"Okay, you sleep and when you wake up we can talk about what's going on. Sound good?" She nods and reaches out to cup my jaw and I grab her hand and press a kiss to it. "We're in this together. I'm not going anywhere."

She smiles at me, not a full-blown grin but the kind that accompanies the heavy droop of her eyelids. I kiss her palm again and tuck her in as she falls asleep.

I take the scrubs into the bathroom with me and change quickly, mouthing a silent thank you to Susan when she takes my pile of wet things from me. I watch her leave and close the door behind her and pull the recliner chair closer to Carlisle's bed so I can watch her sleep. I grab my backpack and pull out my textbook, opening it to the reading for tomorrow.

My phone buzzes and I pick it up, groaning at the text on the screen.

We are here for group. Where are you?

I stare at the gray box on my phone and glance at Carlisle. She's out cold and probably will be for hours if not the rest of the night. The PT sessions wear her out and today's reaction could just be the result of fatigue.

Or it could be something worse and I won't know until she wakes up and I can persuade her to talk to me. Her red-gold hair is drying on the pillow around her face. The freckles on her nose are visible in her too pale face. She's thinner now but not enough for me to be really worried, but it doesn't take a rocket scientist to figure out that she's carrying around a lot of shit in her head.

I start typing. *Can't make it tonight. Something came up. Sorry.*

I don't have to wait long for a reply. *I hope you know what you're doing. Don't miss lecture asshole.*

I toss my phone into my bag and settle back in the seat, my book unopened on my lap as I look at her. I know what

I'm doing. Carlisle is my world and she needs me now. No matter how important school is, she has to come first.

Chapter Twenty

Carlisle

It is dark outside when I wake up and the digital clock by my bed says "2:15 am".

The room is quiet, the facility deep in collective REM as I blink the sleep away from my eyes. I stretch, flexing my arms, my torso and then it hits when my legs barely respond to my command. Like two heavy logs weighing me down into the mattress, the limbs that once propelled me through the water faster than anyone else on the planet have failed me again.

A snore, soft and low, draws my attention and I shift to the left and see Mateo sleeping in the recliner by the side of my bed. His head thrown back, long neck exposed and dark stubble on his chin. He looks delicious and I would love to walk over there and kiss all that exposed skin. I miss touching him, feeling all of his hot skin on mine.

I want him but I don't even feel like myself anymore.

"Hey baby. Why are you awake?"

His voice surprises me and I laugh in half surprise and half shock, smiling when his grin flashes me from across the room. I reach out my hand before I even know I'm doing it and he smiles even more, closing the book on his lap and unfolding his long, lean body from the chair. He crosses the gap in two steps and then he's there and I'm lifting the sheet and he slides in next to me. It's a tight fit but I love it.

He settles in beside me, placing his right arm under my head and looping the other around my waist. We are cocooned together underneath the thin, white, over-bleached sheets and it feels wonderful. He's hard and warm and every part of me fits with him. It's like we were meant to be together. In this moment, I almost feel... whole.

Mateo leans over and kisses me. Once on the right side of my mouth. Once on the left side of my mouth. And finally on my lips, soft and sweet but thorough with a deep sweep of his tongue. I kiss him back, my fingers tangling in his hair and pulling him closer until we have to break for air. We stare at each other for a while, enjoying the closeness. With all the people constantly surrounding me, we haven't had much time to just be together. This is beyond nice but I can't help but notice the fatigue sitting heavily on his shoulders. The slump matches the dark shadows under his eyes. My man looks good but tired, bone-deep tired.

"Why are you still here?" I ask, playing with the fabric of his scrubs. "Why are you wearing these?"

"My clothes got wet and Susan gave these to me." He glances down at himself and then grins back up at me. "I'm trying them on for size. Do you think I look like a doctor?"

I pretend to take my time answering but he looks hot. "You look fuckable-in-the-on-call-room hot."

"Yeah?"

"Oh, yeah." I poke him in the chest. "But you won't ever be 'Dr. Hottie' if you don't get decent sleep and study time. You are always here."

Mateo tenses next to me and I look closely at his face. He avoids my eyes for a few seconds but when he looks back, I only see determination in them.

"I want to be here with you. I want to help you." He traces a finger down my cheek and I lean into it. "I need to be here."

"I have a posse of professionals who are here to help me." As soon as I say this I feel him stiffen again and I sigh, knowing I have hurt him even though I didn't mean to. He looks away and I have to pull his face back around to get him to look at me. "Teo, I want you here. I need you."

"I'm not so sure," he whispers and them almost immediately shakes his head. "Forget it. I shouldn't have said that." He stares at me, clearly thinking of what he wants to ask me. "What happened today?"

Now it's my turn to break eye contact but he doesn't let me get away with it. His finger under chin tips my face up for a quick, sweet kiss before he whispers, "Tell me. I need to know what's going on in your head."

I laugh. It's short and bitter and makes my throat hurt. Or maybe that's the emotion burning its way up from my gut.

"I work so hard and nothing is happening. I do everything they tell me to do. I follow every instruction to the letter and I don't feel any different than I did a month ago." I lean forward and bury my face in his neck, inhaling the comforting scent of my lover. "I'm scared Teo. Nothing works. I can't feel... anything."

I am not exaggerating. Nothing below my waist works right now. I have to empty my bladder and my bowels with enemas and catheters and my vagina and clitoris have gone the way of Elvis and left the building. I should be able to talk to Teo about this but I can't. Not yet. I'm not ready to admit that I might never be the woman he needs. The one he deserves.

"If I tell you everything, it will make it real," I murmur against his throat, pressing a kiss there to ease the sting of not telling him what he wants to hear. "It's just hard and I can't turn off the shit in my head."

"Have you called Dr. Shrieve?"

I shake my head.

"Not yet." I pause and pull back to look at him, willing him to understand and not run from the head case I am obviously morphing into. "But I will. I think I need to talk to her."

"I wish you would talk to me but I get it if you need to work it out with her first. All of this shit is scary."

"Are you scared?"

"Of you conquering this?" He shakes his head, his smile sweet. "No way. You'll kick its ass."

"No. About school. Tell me how it's going."

"It's fine," he says but his lack of eye contact makes me

poke him in the side again. He sighs. "It's hard as shit but fascinating. I'm still waiting for it to feel real, though."

"I think it's because you're never there."

"Here we go," he says on a groan while he presses his forehead against mine. "I'm there plenty. I'm studying and doing fine."

We lie there in silence for a while and I can't pinpoint why I don't believe him. Medical school is hard. I know because I watched ER for all fifteen seasons and it was brutal in make-believe land. He cannot be doing what he needs to do and be here all the time.

"Teo, I can't worry about you messing up school because of me." I pause and then decide to tell him the truth that I can. "I'm going to be selfish and just put it out there that I can't handle one more thing on my plate. Besides the obvious question of whether my body will ever work again, I worry about my parents and Livvy and so many other things that I shouldn't but I do. I just can't worry about your school as well."

He stares down at me, his eyes searching my face in the semi-darkness.

"I need you to do this for me," I plead. "Take this thing off my mind. Please."

He sighs. "What do you need me to do?"

"Go to class. Don't come here every day. Sleep in your own bed and get rid of the dark circles under your eyes. Take time to study properly in a library. Come see me when you can on weekdays and then bug the shit out of me on weekends."

"I want to be *here*."

"And I love you for that but I need to focus on what I need to do and I can't do that if I don't know you're taking care of your business as well." I cup his face in my hand, running my thumb over his cheekbone. "I'm a control freak so give me one less thing to control. Please. Promise me you'll do this."

We have a stare off and I wonder if he'll fight me on it.

I'm stubborn but he's just as bad. I release my breath when he nods, his voice low and resigned as he agrees.

"I'll do it."

"Thank you." I lean up and kiss him, letting our touches linger, enjoying the quiet and each other. My heart thuds in my chest, heavy and slightly elevated with the way he makes me feel. "I've missed you."

"*Tesoro.*" Teo hums against my lips and then traces a path across my cheek to nuzzle into my neck, inhaling deeply. I squirm when it tickles and he laughs softly against my skin. "I've missed you so much. Missed this."

I can't help the thought that passes through my mind. It isn't the first time it's been a visitor in the middle of the night: the question of how we will do this, whether he will want me when I finally have to accept a life of catheters, enemas. Countless trips to every kind of doctor imaginable. A partner confined to a wheelchair.

The definitive verdict of no children. No family.

I always resolve to talk to Mateo about this stuff in the morning but I chicken out. My mother isn't right about everything but she is accurate when she says we haven't had a lot of time to get to know the stuff about each other that comes with being together for a long time. The kind of time that makes you fearless to ask anything and the confidence to know that the answer will not change what exists between the two of you.

We do not have that confidence. We needed more time but we didn't get it and I'm not brave enough to ask.

So I let the moment pass as I lie in the dark and eventually fall asleep and dream of days when I will walk by his side.

Chapter Twenty-One

Carlisle

"What do you want to talk about?" Dr. Shrieve asks from the sofa in my room.

The morning after the night with Mateo I called her and asked for her to come see me at the facility. It wasn't typical for her to leave her office to see a patient and I am grateful she is willing to help me out.

"I don't know." I twist the tie on my sweats and shrug. "Everything."

"Let's narrow it down a little bit, I've only got an hour," she teases before she pulls out the ever-present notebook and looks at me for a full thirty seconds. "You look good. Not great but good. I think you need more sleep."

"I fall asleep and then I'm up a few hours later."

"Maybe you need to take something," she muses as she writes something on the page. "Just to help you sleep better."

"I feel like I'm becoming one big pill. I don't want to shove another one in me."

She nods. "I can get you a prescription for medical marijuana. If I recall it was one of your favorites."

That makes me laugh and I slip her the bird as she answers me with a devious chuckle. It felt weird since she walked in but with this exchange, it feels normal. I spent the last year sharing more with her than with my own family and I think I missed it.

"Well, if you are turning down the chance for pot brownies, let's figure out what's keeping you up." She pauses and looks at me. "I'm presuming it isn't pain-related?" When I shake my head 'no', she continues. "How are you handling all of this? It's a huge change from where you planned to be

147

and so much work."

I stop and think, rolling around what's been in my head since I woke up from the surgery. Should I have just taken the pill stash hidden in my apartment and avoided the whole mess? Saved people a lot of trouble? "I'm not sure that I picked the right choice."

"Okay. Do you plan on changing your mind?"

I think about it. Could I take all those pills now? "I've considered it…but no. I don't think I can now. I'm too invested, people are too invested."

"What do you think the outcome will be in the end? Will you walk? Wheelchair?"

I flinch at her words. They are too raw. Too direct. Everyone has been tiptoeing around me, even when my PT people are killing me, they are achingly polite. This stings but I lean into it. I need this, I think.

"I have no idea and it is making me fucking nuts." I smack the armrest on my wheelchair and the reverberating pain in my hand is sharp but I don't care. "Before I had this surgery I had pain, I hurt all the time and I thought I would do anything to have it gone." I grip my knee in my hand and it's the same light pressure I've felt for the last couple of weeks. "But this feeling nothing is killing me."

I start crying and Dr. Shrieve's eyebrows shoot up. In all our sessions I never cried, never broke down and now I can't seem to stop.

"My body is my enemy. The bombers were my besties compared to the shit my body puts me through on a daily basis. I can't walk. I barely have any feeling from the waist down and I can't even pee by myself." I suck in a huge breath and continue, saying the thing that wakes me and won't let me go. "Everyone keeps telling me that the girl who won all those medals can beat this but what they don't realize is that those goddam medals belong to a girl who should have died along with Aaron and everyone else."

The silence is profound but she keeps her gaze on mine as I gulp, and sniffle, and hiccup my way through the worst of it. And when I begin my descent, she gets up from her seat, walks over to the vanity and picks up the box of tissues. She returns to me and hands it over but instead of going back to her seat, she kneels down and takes my hand in hers.

"You are not that girl. A vital part of her did die that day right next to Aaron and that's okay. It's okay to be mad about it and to resent it and to wish like hell you could have her back." She squeezes my hand and I cling to her like she's a life raft because fuck knows I feel like I'm drowning. "But not all of her is gone. The part that makes you a fighter is there. I've read your medical records from that day and you should have been dead. There is no reason you are sitting here today except that you are a fighter, down deep in your overly competitive, pain-in-the-ass bones, you fight until you can't get up again." And then she smiles at me and pats my hand as she rises. "What I don't understand is why you think this should be easy or you should know the outcome. Learning to break every world record was not easy and every time you got on that block, you had no idea how the race would end. Get in position, wait for the buzzer and jump off the damn block. Be that girl."

She sits back down across from me and watches me as I process everything she said. I want to tell her to fuck off. To yell that she has no idea how hard this is but it doesn't matter. Nobody but me knew how hard every stroke through the water was. How difficult it was to get out of bed some mornings and spend hours in a chilly pool. Yes, they sympathized but they didn't know. It was my fight then and this is my fight now.

I've just got to decide to fight, to focus. I might win gold or I might not place. It's always a crapshoot after all the hard work is done. She's right, this is no different.

"You good?" She asks. I nod and she reopens the notebook. "Who are you talking to about this? What's your support like?"

I shrug. "My parents are here, hovering. I don't want to tell them everything because it freaks them out and they just

149

hover more. I end up wasting energy being annoyed and not putting it into my PT."

"So, you're still trying to take care of everyone around you and not letting them take care of you."

This is well-covered territory for us. Apparently it is not uncommon for someone in an extreme health situation to want to take care of everyone around them by hiding how they are really doing and putting on a brave front. I am not unique in this but I am the poster child according to Dr. Shrieve.

"And Mateo?" she asks when it becomes clear that I'm not going to answer.

This is where it really gets hard. I let out a breath and get really honest.

"I love him but I can't talk to him about this. He's got so much going on and I don't want to burden him."

"Is that how you see yourself? A burden?"

I think about her question. Is that how I see myself?

"Yes. I do."

"Does he see you that way?"

I shake my head. "No. Not yet."

"But you think he will?"

"When we got together he knew nothing about all of this. It all happened so fast, before we really got the chance to know each other, to hash this out. It's like I lured him in under false pretenses and now he's stuck with me. He's too much of a gentleman to back out."

"Have you talked to him about this? How do you think he'd react if he heard this?" she asks.

"He'd deny it. He'd keep trying to do everything and be everywhere. I made him promise to not be here during the week so much, to go to class, to forget about me." I look down at my lap and twist the tie on my sweats again, facing my fear. The boogeyman under my bed. "I'm afraid that he'll mess this up and resent me when he finally gets the courage to leave one day."

Dr. Shrieve stares at me across the short distance. "You

two need to talk about this."

"I know."

"Can you do that if I give you homework? Will you pick one thing and talk to him about it this weekend? You won't know each other better if you don't talk about it." She glances at the clock and closes the notebook. "Build the trust and let the rest follow. Even soul mates have to work at it. You wouldn't be worrying about this if you didn't love him but it's not the most important thing anyway."

"It isn't?"

"No, because even the biggest love won't survive if you don't have the foundation to support it. Work on that, forge that bond and you'll work it out."

She leaves and I sit there in my room, watching the birds and butterflies moving in the courtyard. It's a beautiful view and it helps me focus on what she said and what I have to do.

"Did you have a good session?" my mother asks as she enters the room, the ever-present knitting project in her hands. I have more scarves and mittens than I will ever need. She used to bring them along to my practices and competitions and I could always count on looking up in the stands and seeing my mom, the needles clicking away.

"I did. I like Dr. Shrieve better than the counselor here."

"I'm not surprised, you have a history with her." My mom stops and peers under the bed, squinting as she squats down to get a better look.

"What's up?" I turn my wheelchair, trying to see what she's looking at. I can't help her so I sit in place and watch her drop down on her hands and knees. She stretches her arm and sits up with a folded piece of paper in her hand. She opens it and glances at the top. "It's from Mateo's school."

I take it when she hands it out to me and I open it without thinking. The first couple of lines catch my attention. I know it's not my mail and I have no business reading the entire thing but I read every single word. It's like a car wreck on the side of the road, no matter how many times you tell yourself to get your eyes back on the road, the rubberneck is impossible to resist.

I read it again but the words don't change. Mateo is in danger of flunking out of school. Because he's here with me. At least he was. It's been a week.

"What is it?"

I look up and my mother is giving me the eyeball and I debate telling her the truth. I shake my head and refold the letter, rolling over to my desk and place it inside my planner.

"Nothing."

Nothing but another thing for me and Mateo not to talk about.

Chapter Twenty-Two

Mateo

I walk into Carlisle's room exhausted after the week I just endured but excited to see her.

She's in her wheelchair, looking out the window into the courtyard and I sneak up behind her and bend down to kiss her on the cheek. She leans into me but doesn't respond in her usual way and I move around to her front and kneel down to get an eyeball-to-eyeball view of her face.

"*Tesoro*, you okay?" She looks fine but I quickly scan over her body to see if I can detect any injury, any change. We talk every night but its hard not seeing her everyday. I've got news she isn't going to like but Ill hold it if she's not up for it. "Rough day?"

"I'm fine. I had a good day. It was hard but good, I think," she says, reaching up a hand to stroke my jaw. I lean into like a cat, craving her touch like I've been without it for years instead of just five days.

"Good. I'm glad to hear it." I lean and kiss her mouth, delving in deep with my tongue. I capture her gasp and retreat, lightly biting her lower lip before I let it loose. When I pull back, her eyes are closed and she looks like the Carlisle lying in the back seat of my car or on my bed that morning when this all really began. I am counting the days when we can be there again. "There you are. I've missed you Carlisle Queen."

She gazes at me, her green eyes dark and swirling with whatever has her mouth forced into a thin line. I know it's coming but I still clench my hand around the armrest of her wheelchair.

"We need to talk, Teo."

"The worst four words any man ever wants to hear," I

try to joke but it sounds flat even to my own ears.

She reaches down and takes out a folded letter and I know what it is before she opens it. It must have fallen out of my backpack.

"Why didn't you tell me about this?"

"I didn't want you to worry. You have enough on your mind."

"You should have told me."

She pushes her chair away from me and I immediately feel the distance between us that has grown over the past few weeks. I would expect it to leave me feeling cold but what it creates is a burning sensation in my chest as if the link between the two of us stretched to its limits.

"I didn't want you to worry."

"You said that," her tone isn't ugly but it is unhappy and frustrated. "I'm not fragile Mateo. I'm broken and fucked up but I'm not a child that you have to protect from the hard things."

"Stop putting words in my mouth. I never said or thought any of those things about you."

"Really? Come on Mateo, you didn't tell me because you thought I couldn't handle it."

"You have enough on your mind," I'm firm on this point. "I do not want to be one more thing you have to worry about."

She raises her voice for the first time, her cheeks pink from her high emotion. "I thought we were in this together. Isn't that what you're always saying?

I stand up and pace across the room, crumpling the paper in my hand and lobbing it at the trash can. I turn back to her and try to keep my voice calm. I feel like she's spoiling for a fight and I don't want to rise to the bait. It will get us nowhere to let this devolve into anger and hurtful words but she has to realize that it goes both ways.

"You can't throw that back in my face Carlisle. How many times have I asked you about what is going on, what you're feeling and you shut me out?" I slash my hand through the air and then rake my fingers through my hair. "There are so many topics you have declared off limits that I'm not sure we really have anything to discuss unless you want to stick to the weather. If we're talking about who's shutting who out, then let's take a good look at you too."

"Are you still in danger of being kicked out of a school?"

I stare at her, my mouth hanging open at the way she has completely ignored my comment.

"Just tell me how you are doing in school," she grinds out at me, it's dark and guttural and indicates just how upset she is with me.

"How was *your* day? " I ask, letting the sarcasm drip from every syllable. "And don't tell me it was fine."

She sighs and wipes a hand over her face and she takes a few seconds to bring it down a notch. When Carlisle looks at me again, her voice is softer, more controlled.

"I'm not sure I can do this right now."

I hear the fatigue in her voice and it stops my temper from rising any further. As much as she doesn't want to admit it, she is fragile and her focus can't be distracted by outside things.

"You're right." I agree, moving to sit down on the sofa near he. I reach out to take her hand in my own. "We can talk about this when we aren't both on edge."

She doesn't squeeze my hand back, in fact her grip is loose in mine. I search her eyes, not liking what I see.

"I think I need to go somewhere and just focus on getting better," she whispers and I think I didn't hear her right.

"Go somewhere? What are you talking about?" But I know. I know exactly what she's doing. I just need to hear it.

"I'm going to transfer to another facility for my rehab." The expression on her face looks pained but determined and my stomach sinks into my toes. "Not in Nashville."

"Where would you go?"

"I think I need a clean slate. Nothing on it but getting better. I feel like I've got too many things weighing on me and

I can't concentrate." Her voice sounds dejected, flat. It's as if she has the weight of the world on her shoulders. "I'm going to go, Mateo."

"Carlisle," I say, swallowing hard to get around the boulder lodged in my chest. It's painful and I have trouble sucking in oxygen. My skin is clammy with fear. "Are you breaking up with me?"

She starts crying at my question. Big, fat tears rolling down her cheeks as she sobs quietly, little hiccups of emotion breaking out from between her lips. She has a death grip on my hand and I wonder why she is doing this if it is so damn painful.

"I think the biggest joke in the universe is finding the right person at the wrong time," she whispers and my blood runs cold with her meaning. "I love you but I can't stand the thought of you walking away from me one day." She lets go of my hand and scrubs the tears from her face with the back of her hand. "The only thing worse is that one day you're going to realize what a burden I am but you're going to stay anyway."

"I would never do that," I insist, angry that she is placing behavior and thoughts on me that are not mine. But clearly, they have been rolling around in her head. "I love you and I don't care if you are in a wheelchair or running marathons. I just want you."

"I want that to be true."

"It is true."

"You say that now because you're an honorable man but when you flunk out of med school and throw away this opportunity, you will resent me."

I stand, unable to sit and have this conversation one minute longer.

"Stop putting words in my mouth," I argue. "This isn't how I feel. You've got to stop this soundtrack of negativity going round and round in your head."

"It's how I feel Mateo. It's what keeps me up at night and keeps me from paying attention in physical therapy. It's real and it's hurting me."

"You think that I'm part of the reason you're not making physical progress?"

"I think worrying you and school and how my treatment is taking over everyone's lives and how I feel like I'll be double failure if I never get out of this chair is making me crazy. I'm a mess. It's eating me from the inside out and I just don't have it in me to fight it out on multiple fronts." She takes a deep breath and when she continues. "When I was training, everything else fell to the side. Things that took up too much headspace had to go and I was ruthless about making the hard call. I'm making it now. I need to go somewhere else and immerse myself in my recovery."

She's crying now and I know from her tones that she has her mind made up.

"I love you—"

"Then don't fucking do this," I say, the words like knives in my throat. "I love you too."

"I love you but I have to go and I'm not asking you to wait and I know if I come back, you may have moved on. I know this isn't fair."

"There is nothing about this situation where you make all the decisions about ending us is fair." I struggle to keep my voice down, everyone in this place does not need to witness the moment where my whole fucking world comes to an end. "You cannot do this."

"I'm sorry."

"You said that."

"I hate it but it's what I need to do," she looks up at me, her agony etched on her face but I don't have it in me to touch her, to comfort her. I'm in pain and contact at this point would bring me to my knees. "I'm not asking you to forgive me."

"Good, because I can't give it to you."

And even though I want to beg and plead for her to change her mind, I walk out of the room and leave. We need to time to cool off. Clearly things have come to a head and now that she's gotten this off her chest, we'll talk about calmly later. I'll come back tomorrow. This is not how we end.

Chapter Twenty-Three

Mateo

Ten months later

I am late. Again.

My family and friends have gotten used to my constant state of incurable tardiness. I get caught up in the lab or my volunteer work at the clinic and the clock and little stuff like food and sleep become irrelevant. To my surprise the clinic is the most common culprit. The patients lined up in the waiting room, needy for free medical care grab me and it takes almost no effort to get me to work a few extra hours. Nobody is more shocked about this development than I am.

But the work keeps my mind off of the topic that is absolutely never discussed in my presence. Yeah, I know they spend hours hashing over how I'd buried myself in school when Carlisle left me. They'd given me my space, tip-toeing around the almost-mute asshole I'd been and then thrown about a dozen women at me in an effort to get me to move on. I'd finally caved, going out with a woman named Anne Price, a junior librarian at the Nashville Public Library my mother knew through some ESL class she helped coordinate.

I had intended for our first date to be our last but then she got me to laugh with her pitch perfect Monty Python quotes at dinner and we kept laughing when we tumbled onto her bed two hours later. That was three months ago and we're still together, seeing each other a couple of times per week and never letting our conversation venture past the here and now. But lately she's gotten this look in her eye after we both come; the look that tells me she wants me to say something other than "fuck, that was good" before we roll over and go to sleep.

Anne is shit out of luck. That isn't going to happen.

"Something more" has run me over like a fucking freight train once already and I'm not stupid enough to jump back on the tracks again.

Anne hasn't given me the ultimatum yet but I know it's coming sooner than later. I've never lied to her about what we are and what I can offer her, so she knows what my answer will be. But it hasn't happened yet and so tonight I'm running late for our mid-week dinner date with some of her friends and I still need to drop some stuff off for Kit from my mother.

I pull into the driveway of Max and Kit's house, nodding at the extra hands they have working on the old farmhouse and the large, landscaped yard. The nauseatingly happy couple will be married in the gardens later this summer when Kit returns from her tour and all the home improvements are on hyper speed. I lend a hand as often as I can but that isn't happening tonight.

I snag the box of invitations from the backseat and take the front steps two at a time, skidding to a stop on the doormat and hitting the doorbell. I glance around me, noticing for the first time the silver Volvo parked on the driveway to the left of the house. I don't recognize it or the license plate and I throw up a silent prayer they have company so that I have an excuse to keep my moonlighting as a UPS man as brief as possible.

Max opens the door and his usual smile does not appear. He doesn't even say hello. "Oh shit" is all he gets out before he glances over his shoulder towards the large family room off the main foyer and I see someone sitting on their sofa.

No. Not someone.

Carlisle.

"Oh shit" tumbles past my own lips as her gaze tracks to the door and locks with mine. Even at that distance I can see the widening of her eyes, the perfect "o" formed by her mouth.

I drop the box in my hands and grab the doorframe. I sway a little on my feet and wonder for a split second if I will be able to maintain the last shreds of my dignity and remain on my feet. Shocked. Gobsmacked. Blindsided. You pick the term you like best and that is me.

"Mateo... man, I am so sorry. If I'd known you were coming over, I would have warned you," Max says as he reaches out to catch me just in case I decide to take a header onto his newly refinished oak floors. "I'm sorry, man."

I just stare at her, soaking in every detail. Her hair is longer, still the same deep, rich red with the streaks of gold shining in the sunlight streaming through the huge windows I helped Max install. One look at her and I realize that the Carlisle that still haunted my dreams is a fucking poor imitation of the real thing. She is amazing. Gorgeous. Beautiful.

And my traitorous fucking heart keeps trying to jump out of my chest and get to the woman who'd taken it with her when she left the rest of me behind.

"Mateo. You okay?" Max's voice penetrates through the fog of "what-the-hell" that has taken over my brain and I drag my gaze back to his face.

"Yeah." I shake my head and bend down to pick up the box I dropped, keeping my eye on Carlisle in my peripheral vision. "My mom finished the calligraphy on the wedding invitations for Kit and..."

I barely register Max taking the box from my hands as Carlisle's movements catch my eye. She's rising from the couch, her actions careful, a little jerky but executed with purpose as she pulls over two forearm crutches and rises to her feet. Everything about her muscle tension, the way she bites her bottom lip, and the familiar bunching of her eyebrows testify to her concentration as she straightens and balances herself on her own two feet.

My breath catches in my throat and I know the sound that escapes from my mouth is harsh and wet with the emotion that threatens to break free.

I've never seen anything look so fucking good in my whole life.

At least I think so until she starts to walk towards me, her steps a little slower than her usual stride but strong and sure. I'd have to be a bigger asshole than I am to deny that the sight of her walking is like Christmas and my birthday and every fucking Fourth of July fireworks display I have ever seen or would ever see.

Carlisle's half smile is tentative, only her eyes giving away her doubt and all the emotion zinging back and forth between us. Somewhere in my head, I knew I would see her again and I knew it would be charged with everything we'd had between us at one time and all the things we would never have. But this actual moment is a million times crazier. Harder. Better. Worse. Amazing. Painful.

The ache starts in my gut and expands, sending out stinging tendrils pulsing out in time with the throbbing of my heart. After ten months I've gotten to the point where I can push it to the back of my mind and push on through. I get up in the morning. I go to work. The twinge is always there and I was reminded frequently enough to ensure that I never did feel "normal". It made sure I never forgot.

So, no matter how good she looks. No matter how glad I am that she is doing well, I can't afford to forget what she did to us. What she did to me.

She wrecked me. I went back to the rehab facility the next day and she was gone. All of her stuff packed. No forwarding address. Her phone turned off. And if I hadn't had my family and Zane to kick my ass, I might have stayed down on the ground where she'd left me.

Kit trails along behind her, stopping to stand next to Max with the best seats in the house to witness whatever this was going to be.

"Hello Mateo," Carlisle says, her voice soft but clear in the unnaturally hushed foyer. She glances down when she has to adjust her grip on her crutches but when she looks back up at me, her smile has more strength and purpose but doesn't disguise the nervous edge to her voice. "It's so good to see you. You were on my list of people to see now that I've moved back to Nashville."

"Well, it's nice to know I made the list." My tone is harsher than I intended, the effort it takes to push words past all the emotional shit clogging up my chest making the edges ragged. And I'm pissed. Fucking white-hot angry and it must have shown on my face because her upper body reels back a little bit, her emerald green eyes wide with her surprise.

"We'll leave you two alone for a few moments," Kit murmurs as she tugs on Max's arm and leads him out of the room and back into the family room. I don't care if they stay or not. Anybody who has any doubt about how this is going down is a fool.

"Teo, I know you're angry…" Carlisle begins but I'm not having any of it.

"Wow. I'm allowed to have feelings or an opinion or anything with you around? I thought you had the monopoly on making decisions for both of us. I was ready to sit back and wait for you to tell me how to react when after *ten fucking months* of radio silence you show up at my cousin's house and tell me that I was on your list of goddam people to see when you prance your *royal highness* ass back into town."

My voice doesn't need the awesome acoustics of this old house to relay just how pissed off I am. Months of holding it in, sending emails to an account that bounces them back to me, and calls to a number that is never answered erupts in my speech. I regret nothing.

Not. One. Word.

Carlisle's cheeks turn a vivid shade of pink with her reaction, anger, embarrassment or something else, I have no idea. I don't trust my read on her anymore, not after she blindsided me with her one-sided decision for us to be over. Her grip on her crutches is white knuckle and her entire body vibrates with whatever is going on in her head.

"You were first on my list. The person I wanted to see the most."

"That explains you being *at Max and Kit's house*. I'm sure you got confused that I don't actually live here." I'm not giving an inch. No way am I making this easy on her. "Well, you can check me off the list and consider us caught up."

She steps forward, everything about her demeanor screaming how rattled she is but she pushes on in typical Carlisle fashion. I can't help the admiration and the spike of attraction that hits me in the gut. If I'd tried to kid myself that I was over her, it wasn't working.

"Teo, you were *first* on the list." Carlisle takes a deep breath and blurts out the rest in a voice barely above a whisper. "But I had to build up the nerve to come see you. I—"

"Did you think I was going to bite or something?" I walk towards her, close enough that she has to lift her face to look at me and close enough for me to smell her scent. The familiar smell of her gardenia soap envelopes me and I have to close my eyes for a moment, steeling myself against the rush of memories that accompanies it. I remember the day when I lost that scent on my sheets, in my car, on my clothes and realized she wasn't coming back to me. It was hell, whichever layer Dante reserved for fools. "Or were you afraid that I would lose my shit? Yell? Break something?"

She shakes her head, emerald eyes huge as she stares at me. I'm staring so hard right back that I don't even see her reaching out to touch me until her cool fingers brush against the skin on the back of my hand. My instinct is to extend my fingers and weave them together with hers, to pull her close and stop all this useless talk with the press of my lips against her own.

"No. I was afraid you wouldn't... " She stumbles on her words and I can hear the effort it takes for her to swallow down whatever is caught in her throat. "I was... " She corrects herself and starts over again. "I am afraid that you're going to tell me it's too late. That I'm too late and we're over."

I've spent nights, days, countless minutes praying for her to show up and say exactly what she just said. Longing, not just for her body or for sex, but the *need* for her to fill this Carlisle-shaped hole in my chest almost knocks me down. My mouth waters, my heart kicks into a beat that rivals a Red Hot Chili Peppers song, and sweat prickles between my shoulder blades. I'm a mess and I hate it. I hate that this is my reaction after all those fucking months, after she walked out and left me hanging with more questions than answers, after she acted so selfishly. I hate... her.

As much as I ever loved her, I hate her now. In this moment. Right fucking now.

"It's too late," I say and pull my hand away. I keep my eyes glued to hers because I want to see her reaction to my words. I want to see the pain I hope I'll inflict. It's not pretty and it's not nice but it's real. "I'm with someone else."

"Oh." She blinks rapidly and I can see the extra moisture filling them as she sucks in a ragged breath. "Are you... do you... ?"

"I love her." I answer the question she can't get out and I close my eyes against the pain that flares in her own and sends a flush of red heat over her porcelain skin. I immediately want to take it back, to rewind and delete the lie. Carlisle and I never lied to each other. Even when we said stuff that neither of us wanted to hear, we always told the truth. This is wrong. "Carlisle... "

My phone rings, the ringtone loud in the silence that has surrounded us. I fish it out of my pocket and glance at the screen. Anne.

"You take that. I'm sure it's important," Carlisle says as I swipe the screen to send the call to voicemail.

"Carlisle. Wait—" I shove the cell back in my pocket and try to capture her hand with my own but she's already stepping backwards and turning towards the family room.

"It was great to see you Teo... Mateo. I'm glad you're doing so well." She pauses in her retreat and gives me one of those smiles you know is fake only because you know the person so well. It won't convince me and she knows it but this whole scene is now about saving face and acting like nothing between us ever happened. We aren't Carlisle and Mateo anymore. We're just people who used to fuck and share and tried to make each other happy. Strangers. "And I'm so glad you're happy. Really glad."

For a split second I think about following her but I don't. I might feel like an asshole for throwing out the whole "I love her" lie but nothing has changed. Carlisle is still the woman who makes me stop breathing but I can't forget what she did. Why would I do that to myself again? It's pride and ego and all that male bullshit but it's all I've got right now.

The hate I felt was real. As real as how much I still love her. I don't know how you get past that. I'm not sure I want to.

I turn and open the door, not even bothering to yell a goodbye towards Max and Kit. They'll figure out that I'm gone with one glance into the foyer. Besides, we're family and you can forget your manners with blood relatives and they have to take it. It's a rule.

I get to my car, slamming the door as I settle behind the wheel, my hands clenching at ten and two. I glance up at myself in the rearview mirror, my pupils are blown as if I'm high or aroused. Or angry. Emotional. Freaking the fuck out.

Where is the multiple choice answer for "all of the above"?

I pull out of the driveway and head towards downtown Nashville and the trendy, microbrew restaurant where I'm having dinner with Anne and her friends. Traffic is light and it's a good thing because I'm on autopilot, navigating the turns, the lane changes, and the speed limits with my mind very preoccupied with what just happened.

Carlisle is here and she's staying.

And while my head actually hurts with that mind-blowing truth another one pops in that threatens my ability to breathe.

She can walk.

Wherever she'd gone, whatever she'd done all these months, had worked. She was walking, with the aid of crutches, but she'd beaten the odds and made a comeback. It was all I wanted for her, no matter what happened between us.

As I pull into the parking area for the restaurant and hand over my keys to the attendant, the memory of Carlisle moving towards me would not banish itself to the background. I should not be thinking of her, should not linger over the details of how she looked: a little thinner but still strong, her hair longer and curlier, the same spatter of freckles along the bridge of her nose, the same cool fire in her emerald green eyes.

"Mateo." I am ripped out of my little fantasy by Anne striding towards me, her blonde curls framing her smiling face.

She walks straight to me and loops her arms around my waist, lifting her face for a kiss. This woman is openly affectionate, sweet, and uncomplicated. To fall for her would be easy and our relationship would be smooth and drama-free. I press my lips to hers, willing myself to forget what just happened, to keep Carlisle in my past where she belongs.

"Hey," I say when I end the kiss, hoping my voice sounds normal and not like the bottom just fell out from under me like those rides at the amusement park. "You look good."

She smiles at me but something in my expression makes it falter. "You all right?"

I nod, kissing the top of her head as we turn to walk into the restaurant. "I'm fine."

I look straight ahead as I try to forget the fact that for the first time in our relationship, I just lied to Anne.

Chapter Twenty-Four

Carlisle

"Why didn't we live in a place as nice as this when I was here?"

Livvy gives me a dirty look as she trails her gaze from the gorgeous view of the Nashville skyline to the modern interior of my new apartment. It is a lot nicer than the place we lived in.

"Because I hated you." I smile widely at the middle finger she is pointing in my direction. "I still do."

"Kiss my ass your majesty."

"I have no idea where that ass has been," I toss back at her as I roll myself across the hand-scraped floors to the sofa where I go through the movements necessary to transfer my body to the extra-wide cushions. Balance and strength earned through countless hours of training in a gym make it possible. Livvy watches from her place by the window, her eyebrow raised in the universal silent question of "do you need help?" but I wave her off. It's not the most graceful dismount but I make it there with minimal fuss and only a little breathless. "I loved our old place but this building has better accessibility for the wheelchair."

"How often are you in it these days?"

I settle against the armrest and reach out to snag my bottle of soda from the coffee table before I answer. "Lately, I've used the crutches more often but it really depends on what my body feels like doing that day. I still engage with my physical therapist and I work out every day but it varies along with my level of pain. I never know whether I will be in the chair or on the crutches."

She crosses the room and plops down beside me, her

face full of concern. "I thought the pain was going to get better?"

"It's so much better than it was but it's never all gone." I tip the bottle back and take a sip. "I can handle it without drugs for the most part and on the occasions where it is elevated, I have a prescription."

"No more self-medicating then?" I shake my head and she gives me a teasing grin. "You single-handedly put an entire drug cartel out of business by going cold turkey."

I toss a pillow at her face. "Screw you." We settle back into comfortable silence and I get back to her original question. "This building has a place next to the elevator for my car and it's accessible no matter what my condition. I'd love to live in a funky loft with all kinds of weird levels but my independence is more important. From here I can get to school, my gym, my doctor. It works."

"So, school? What are you? The oldest sophomore in the history of Nashville U?"

"I think I might be," I say, thinking about the summer classes I will take to ease back into the life of a student. I'm nervous but not because of the academics or my classmates, it's more elemental. I look at my best friend and I confess. "This will be the first time I will live completely independently since the surgery. When you leave, I will be completely on my own."

"Scary shit," she muses.

"Terrifying but exciting too. I'm ready for it."

"I'm proud of you. I never told you but I am." She smiles but I can see the moisture making her eyes glassy. "And I'm really glad you're still here. I love you and I can't imagine anyone else standing up with me when I get married."

I reach across the couch and grab her hand, squeezing her fingers lightly while I also fight back the bawling that comes so often these days. The barriers I put up after the bombing, after Aaron died, are all gone. Taken away with the little bits of metal from my back and I feel things keenly these day. I'm not a walking/talking blubbering mess but the sensations of joy, sorrow, loss, and appreciation are sharp, clear and run very deep but are also just below the surface of my thin skin.

"I love you too Livvy."

We sniffle and laugh and give our eyes a very unlady-like swipe with our hands before we settle back on the sofa, enjoying the sunshine spilling in through the floor-to-ceiling windows and the view of downtown Nashville. I picked this condo for the view, even when I'm not in it I feel like I'm part of the life and bustle in the streets. Even rattling around in the large two bedroom, two and half bath unit won't feel so lonely when I can look below and see so much vitality and energy.

At least that is the plan.

"Have you seen Mateo yet?" Livvy asks and while the question is abrupt, I was expecting it so I didn't even flinch.

I nod. "I saw him yesterday when I went to Max and Kit's house."

"You went to see them before you went to see *Mateo*?"

"He had the same reaction," I laugh but it tastes and sounds bitter. "I felt like an ass when I saw him. I should have gone to see him right away but it wouldn't have made a difference."

"Why not? It would have shown him that you've been pining for the last ten months." I roll my eyes and she holds up a hand and gives me the "don't even try to deny it" finger wag and head toss. "I said it: pining. Don't you even try to deny it. You were a miserable bitch who took it out on everyone around her."

I wasn't going to deny it but I did have one objection. "I didn't take it out on anyone but I did channel it to make myself work harder."

"Miserable. Bitch." Her lips are in a thin line, telling me that I won't win this argument.

I let it go. Getting down to the heart of the matter... namely the new info I received from Mateo yesterday.

"Well, it doesn't matter anymore. He has a girlfriend and

he's in love with her."

"He told you that?" she asks, her face incredulous. "I throw the bullshit flag."

"I can only believe that it's the truth." I take another sip from my bottle and consider my options. There aren't any. "I'm not a home wrecker so it's got to be the end. I'll see him around but it will have to be as friends."

"That's so wrong."

"I knew when I left that this might be the way it ended. I didn't ask him to wait for me and he didn't. I gambled and I lost."

"You weren't playing a game," she protests. "You did what you thought was right at the time. You guys weren't talking and had shit you needed to figure out."

"It was a gamble no matter what and I lost him." I gaze at the skyline outside the window and wonder where Mateo is out there. I wondered this a million times when I was in Texas but being here in the same city with him makes the longing almost painful. "I wouldn't change it, I wasn't in the right place to be with him but it doesn't make it suck any less."

Livvy scoots over to me on my big, new couch and cuddles up close and we hug, leaning back against the smooshy cushions. She brushes away my tears and kisses my cheek, holding me close as I let go of a dream I've carried around for ten months.

Chapter Twenty-Five

Mateo

The party in the Veranda Room at the Hermitage Hotel is the last place I want to be but Anne is excited enough for both of us.

"I have always wanted to go to a music industry party and I can't believe my first one is here," she gushes and squeezes my hand. "I hope I'm dressed up enough for it."

I glance over her frame, admiring the pale blue cocktail dress that hugs her figure and sets off her blonde hair perfectly. Her cheeks are pink from makeup and her excitement and her smile makes me grin back at her. It is one of the things I like about her, her enthusiasm for life is infectious and she often pulls me out of my moods. I realize that I have been a shit boyfriend tonight and forgotten the most basic of moves.

"You look beautiful. Kit is gonna be pissed when everyone is looking at you and not her."

Anne blushes but leans in for a quick kiss, her "thank you" a little breathless. I'm glad I brought her with me. I've been distant since seeing Carlisle three days ago and Anne has noticed but she hasn't said anything. She wouldn't, it's not her style. So when Kit and Max invited me and a plus-one to her tour kickoff party, I jumped at the chance to make it up to my girlfriend.

"Mateo!" I turn and see Max waving me over from across the room. We make our way to him, entering the Veranda Room with its barrel vaulted ceiling painted to look like the blue sky and the floor-to-ceiling windows that open onto Sixth Avenue. My cousin is dressed similar to me: dark suit with unbuttoned white dress shirt underneath and dark cowboy boots. Nashville formalwear.

"Hey man." We give each other the one-armed bro hug and I watch as he gives Anne a full one and a kiss on the cheek. "Tell Kit thank you for not making us wear monkey suits to this thing."

"God forbid you have to get out of your scrubs for anything," Anne says, poking me in the side.

"You see me get out of scrubs quite often," I tease with a wink and dodge her poking me in the side again. I laugh and leer at Max.

"The less I know about your sex life the better," he says, leading us over to the open bar and placing our drink orders. "We've got a band later for dancing but Kit has a few things to do for the press here at the beginning."

He snags Anne's wine and my whiskey and hands them over and we all take a minute to look around the room. It's packed with band members, record executives, friends, family and the press. Anne spies a friend and leaves us to go and say hello at the same time I see Zane talking to a local magazine. I smile at how easily he rocks the bad boy guitarist thing with the dark hair, black leather pants and the tattoos. And if the way he's smiling down at the cute little reporter, there's probably a good chance I'll see her at breakfast tomorrow morning.

"Zane is so excited to go on tour with Kit. He's been driving me bat shit crazy."

"Those two are going to be trouble on tour because she thinks he's the greatest thing ever. She loves his playing and hopes they'll get to write a bunch of songs together," Max says. "I told him that if I have to bail them out of jail even once, that I will beat his ass and leave the parts for the buzzards to eat."

I laugh and take a sip of my whiskey, starting to relax and suddenly I'm glad I came. I don't see my cousin as often with school and I miss him. "Where is your bride-to-be? She didn't run off with some rock star and leave you hanging?"

"No, you ass." He points over to the side of the room

where Kit is holding court with a group of people. "She's right there."

She's introducing a tall, leggy blonde around to the crowd but I don't recognize her, so I lean in to ask. "Who is that with her?"

Max levels a look at me and shakes his head. "That's Emory Cabell... Kit's half sister."

"What?" I don't even disguise my shock. As far as I know, Kit is an only child. "How did that happen?"

"Well, when two people love each other or just get really drunk, they kiss and take off their clothes... " He trails off when I punch him in the arm.

"Shut the fuck up and tell me how Kit suddenly has a sister."

"Daddy Landry couldn't keep it in his pants and he had a whole other family on one of his regular trucking routes. With Kit's mom gone or on drugs most of the time, nobody blames him but it's still a shock."

"Tell me you got a DNA test."

"We did and it's all legit." He nudges me with his elbow and gives me a "but there's more" look. "She sings like an angel and plays guitar like nobody's business. Kit's taking her on tour as a backup singer."

"Of course she is." And I'm not surprised at all. Kit has the biggest heart and it would never occur to her to shut out family. Anybody who knows what she did for her mom knows what kind of person she is. "I hope Emory is ready for her big sister. Kit can be a little intense."

She's like a fucking hurricane of energy and we all just brace ourselves and go along for the ride.

"They are thick as thieves. It's like they've known each other forever."

I start to ask another question but I'm cut off by the sight of Kit's record label president heading to the small stage and tapping onto the microphone. He welcomes everyone to the party and goes on and on, telling us what we already know: Kit is amazing and this tour is going to make a shitload of money.

He doesn't use those words exactly but that's what we all know he means.

The suit finally gets off the stage and Kit jumps into his space and the room erupts into whistles, catcalls and applause and I join in, adding a loud whoop to the mix.

She rolls through her own speech, thanking her label and introducing her band, including Zane who looks like he's about to explode with excitement, pride or both. Anne joins me again as Kit says she has one more announcement and I slip my arm around her waist. I catch Max giving me a significant look but I was sleeping in the day they gave out instructions on how to read his mind so I have no fucking idea what he is trying to tell me.

I didn't have long to wonder.

Kit is talking so I give her my full attention. "I am really excited to partner with a very special friend of mine on a project that has become near and dear to my heart. I'm going to ask our newest Nashville neighbor and twelve-time gold medalist, Carlisle Queen to join me on stage."

I freeze on the spot, eyes glued to the auburn-haired woman slowly making her way onto the stage to stand next to Kit. She is using her crutches and dressed in a strapless gown the color of rubies and it matches her lipstick. She is fucking gorgeous.

"She really is," Anne agrees with me and I realize that I said it out loud. I bite back another curse at my stupidity. I need to be careful or I might hurt someone who has nothing to do with my history with Carlisle Queen. "I just want to cry when I think about all she's been through. She really loved Aaron Daniels. You could tell by the way they looked at each other that they adored each other."

I have nothing to say to that comment but I wondered if people thought that when we'd been together. I'd fucking worshipped the ground she walked on.

A t-shirt flashes up on the big screen. Black with stylized heart on the front, made of gold rectangles with words written on them: strength, community, hope. In the upper left of the heart is red block with the word "heart" written on it. The front of the tee flashes up and over the heart area is a familiar logo, the "A" and "D" interlocked with waves of water. It's the foundation Carlisle started to honor the memory of her dead lover.

"Carlisle and I designed this t-shirt and it will be on sale at every concert stop and every penny will go to support the Aaron Daniels Foundation and will provide financial support to athletes who wish to compete in the Paralympics." Kit joins the clapping that rises up from the audience. She gestures to Carlisle to step up to the microphone and at first she refuses but she finally gives in and takes the two forward steps necessary to be heard. Her voice is clear, that honey whiskey sound that I hear in my dreams sometimes. More often than I care to admit.

"I want to thank Kit for supporting this project." She pauses and I recognize the crease between her brows as a sign that she is gathering her thoughts. "As you can tell, my mobility has been impaired as a result of the bombing that injured me and ten more and killed twenty-two other athletes, including Aaron. I cannot express how much I have missed competitive athletics but I have wonderful memories of winning gold for my country. The pride I felt in that moment will stay with me the rest of my life. And so to have this opportunity to help other athletes to do the same thing is amazing. Thank you."

Applause rise up again and then dies down as people return to partying. I watch as Kit and Carlisle pose for photos and press the flesh but eventually they leave the stage and a local band takes their place and begins the first set. Many couples spill out on the dance floor as the party kicks up a notch but I can't take my eyes off Carlisle. Every inch of my skin is hyper-aware that she is in the same room and I have to fight the urge to walk across the room and haul her into my arms and kiss the living fuck out of her.

I tense when I notice Kit and Carlisle headed in our direction and I scramble to find a way to pull Anne away when she notices the same thing.

"Oh my God, Kit and Carlisle are coming over here. Max can you introduce me, I have always wanted to meet Carlisle," Anne gushes, her hand squeezing mine.

Max and I exchange a glance and I know he's thinking that I could introduce them. I won't... for obvious reasons.

"You bet," he replies and steps forward to kiss his wife and hug Carlisle. She hasn't noticed me yet but I know the second she does because her whole body stiffens and she bites the bottom of her lip. I almost miss what Max is saying.

"... introduce you to a friend of ours, Anne Price." He pauses just the tiniest second and I wonder how he's going to handle this. "She's Mateo's girlfriend."

Carlisle looks at me then, her green eyes widening with surprise and a tiny bit of hurt but she recovers quickly, her natural ability with people kicking in. She extends her hand to Anne with a warm smile.

"It's nice to meet you Anne. Mateo has told me wonderful things about you."

I haven't told her shit except the lie about loving Anne but I see what she's doing. Keeping it classy and ensuring that Anne isn't caught up in any awkward undertow pulsing between us. I am grateful for her kindness, the pit in my belly loosening a bit.

"I am so excited to meet you, Ms. Queen. I am a huge fan." She turns to look at me with a confused expression on her face. "But I had no idea you knew Mateo."

"I met him when I lived here last year." She glances at me, uncertainty with how much I've told Anne all over her face. I shake my head. I've told Anne nothing. What would be the point? "He was my teaching assistant for freshman Spanish."

I let out the breath I'd been holding. Excellent save Carlisle.

"Oh, Mateo didn't tell me he was a TA for that class but

that's no surprise since he grew up in a bilingual household."

"He was a great TA." She twists her lips in a self-deprecating grin and laughs. "I was a terrible student."

"Is that true Mateo?" Anne places her hand on my chest and I watch Carlisle's gaze lock on the place she's touching. I'd have to be blind to miss the jealousy that skates across her features and the surge of adrenaline it gives me. "I don't believe it."

"She has the worst pronunciation I've ever heard." At my reply Carlisle's eyes snap up to meet mine and I realize that my comment was a mistake because now all I can think about is that first night in my house, in the laundry room, our bodies moving together and the look on her face when she came. I flash hot all over my body and my cock gets hard in my pants.

Fuck.

"Can I get a photo with you?" Anne's innocent question to Carlisle snaps us both back from the place we should not have been and I realize that my girlfriend is holding out her phone to me. "Baby, can you take it for us?"

I take the phone from her and tap the app to activate the camera, willing my body and my mind to get back under control. Carlisle and I are over. I moved on. I need to stay there.

"Say cheese," I tell them and snap a few for good measure before handing the phone back to Anne and accepting a kiss on the cheek in thanks.

Anne excuses herself to go freshen up and Carlisle and I are left staring at each other in a room that is quickly filling up with people. The crowd has pushed us closer to each other and I try not to flinch when her arm brushes my torso. Someone jars her crutches and she pitches forward, into and up against me and I automatically reach out to steady her, my lips brushing the soft curl of her hair as I lean in.

"I think I need to get to a place with fewer people," Carlisle says, her face tipped back to make eye contact with me. This close I can see the freckles on her nose, muted by the thin layer of powder on her skin. She still wears the same perfume; gardenias and sunshine. I'm not the only one feeling what is pulsing between us. Her pupils are large and dark, her neck flushed that pretty shade of pink that happens when she's aroused. I know that if I lean in and touch my lips to the blush, she will be warmer there.

I remember it all.

"Let me get you away from the bar. This area will be mobbed the rest of the night," I say, making sure she's steady on her crutches and waiting for her signal before placing my hand at the small of her back and leading her away. I hover over her, trying to block her from the worst of the crush as I lead her away from that scene and into the area just outside of the Veranda Room.

It's so much quieter here and the lights are dimmer. Along the hallway there are alcoves containing ornately leaded windows and built-in benches with cushions. I lead her over to the nearest one, releasing my hold on her body and giving her space to catch her breath.

The gold tone of the light here highlights the spun gold strands of her hair and the warm space amplifies her scent. I inhale deeply and clench my hands by my side. She's right here in front of me and I could reach out and touch her if I wanted to.

Carlisle's gaze is cast down when she says, "Anne is lovely. I'm very happy for you."

I want to throw back my head and howl at the game we are playing. I don't want her to be happy for me. I don't want her to praise my choice in her replacement. I want answers.

"Why did you come back here? Why didn't you just stay gone?" I ask, my voice gritty with anger and want. She hears it, I can tell by the way the muscles in her back and shoulders tense up but she refuses to make eye contact with me. She keeps her focus on her hands as they smooth out nonexistent wrinkles in her skirt. She ignores me.

"Kit tells me that she's a librarian. I think that's wonderful." Her voice falters and she clears her throat.

"Wonderful."

"Why didn't you contact me? Would it have killed you to tell me where you were going?" I persist, determined to have the conversation I need to have.

We start the ping-pong of questions that only piss me off more and more.

"I love her hair. It's that honey gold that people pay a lot of money to get but I can totally tell she's a natural."

"I waited months for you to call or send an email. It was killing me not to know how you were doing."

"Kit says your mom introduced you two. Carmela has excellent taste."

"I waited and waited until it became clear that you weren't coming back, that you didn't give a shit about me or what I was going through."

"I'm feeling better now. I think I'll go back to the party."

She stands up and I move in closer, blocking her body with my own. I'm a mess of anger, hurt, and desire so poignant that it actually hurts to be in my skin. I reach out a hand and tip her face up to me and groan in pain with what I see there.

Tears. Tracks of wetness down her cheeks and agony in her eyes that takes my breath away.

"I waited and waited for you to come back to me. I missed you... " I swallow hard and try to breathe around the ache in my chest. "... I still miss you. Every second of every day and it's killing me. I'm carrying around all this pain because I'm drowning with the weight of needing you so damn much. I need to feel nothing for you. I love you so much I can't even hate you so I just need to be numb. But I can't." I tip her head back further, loving the feel of her fingers clutching my shirt, nails digging into my skin. We are so close, I feel the vibration of her soft moan against my lips. "So I want an answer to my question, why did you come back here?"

Chapter Twenty-Six

Carlisle

"I came back for you."

I can't lie, not about this. Even though every part of me is screaming for me to deny this truth, I can't. I barely get the words out of my mouth before Mateo is on me, his lips pressing against mine, his tongue pushing for entrance I freely give. It isn't the sweet, tender kiss you would imagine after months spent apart. No, this is rough and brutal and almost painful in its intensity.

I am on fire. My skin is burning, my blood running hot like lava in my veins. I move my hands from his shirt to around his neck, pulling him even closer when he groans like this contact just might kill him.

The slow burn in my belly is amazing, confirming that the sensations that had gradually returned were back and making me ache with need. My own experimentation with fingers and toys has produced orgasms and I am so relieved to experience them again. But they are nothing like his touch and I arch into it, barely registering the clatter of my crutches to the floor at our feet.

I'm not worried about falling. Mateo has me wrapped in his arms and he was holding me tight.

"I missed you so much, *Tesoro*." His words breathed against my cheek make me shiver and I blink back the tears of joy at hearing him call me "his treasure" once again. "I missed you."

"I missed you too."

Laughter erupts behind us as a group of people walk by, reminding me of where we are. Anyone can walk by and see us.

Anne can walk by and see us.

Mateo is not mine.

I lower my hand and push at his chest, ducking my face away when he leans back in for another kiss.

"Stop," I demand, emphasizing my point with a shove. He moves back and I lower myself to the bench behind me, running a hand over my heated cheeks. What had been fiery passion was now nothing but the ache of unfulfilled longing and burning shame. "We are not these people."

There are two beats of silence before he speaks and his voice is heavy and dark. "Fuck."

"We can't do this, Mateo. We shouldn't be doing this at all. What if Anne had seen us?" I raise my face to look at him and see what I know is reflected on my face. "She would be devastated, hurt. We *are not* the people who would do that to someone else."

"You're right Carlisle. You're absolutely right."

His voice breaks and he raises a hand to his face but I see his expression before he covers it up and what I see kills me.

Stricken. Devastated. Broken. Ashamed.

Those words are the first that come to my mind and I feel sick.

"I won't deny that I still have feelings for you Mateo but I don't want what we had to be spoiled by us making it ugly and hurtful."

"Neither do I." He finally looks at me and I can see the pain and confusion in his eyes and etched in the lines on his face. "Anne is a good person."

"She is and now is your time with her. We had our chance, yeah?" I nod and attempt a smile but my lips are too wobbly with the tears I am fighting to hold back. "I think we just need time. Time to adjust."

Time to avoid each other until I don't love him anymore.

"It's just... " He stops and considers his words and I hold my breath, wondering what he will say next. "We just need time."

We stare at each other for several long moments as the

party is happening all around us. In another time we would have been out there with them, holding hands, dancing, kissing. Maybe we would have left the party and come to this very spot for deeper kisses and whispered promises for later. Our being together would have hurt no one and we wouldn't have hurt each other.

"I might have made a mistake coming back to Nashville," I say.

"Don't say that."

"I think it was selfish of me to expect for us to be able to start over or be friends. We have too many people in common to avoid each other and sooner or later this is going to ruin whatever we could hope to salvage."

"I will miss you too much if you go somewhere else," he says, before he kneels down in front of me so we can be eye level. "This is really fucked up right now and I have no clue what I'm doing or what I'm going to do but I don't want you to go. It's selfish and I have no right to ask you but I'm doing it."

My heart squeezes at his words and I feel something else in my chest and I recognize it for what it is: hope. Hope for him to come back to me. Hope that maybe I can learn to be content with just having him in my life. Hope is a bitch. She's the friend who swears to always be there and then ditches your ass when she gets a boyfriend. I hate hope.

I can't afford to have hope where Mateo is concerned because I will always yearn for the thing I cannot have. Somebody has to be the honest one in this crazy mess. It looks like it is me.

"I don't think I can promise you that, Mateo."

He opens his mouth to protest and I brace myself for his protest, but we are interrupted by Max appearing in the opening of the alcove.

"Mateo, Anne is looking... " He sees his cousin at my feet and his eyes grow wide with shock and so many questions. "Is there something wrong? Are you okay Carlisle?"

I muster a smile for him and even pat Mateo on the shoulder like he's a good dog who just obeyed my command to fetch or sit. "The crowd was too much with my crutches so Mateo brought me over here to rest for a bit, but now I think I really just want to get a cab and head home."

Mateo's eyes clash with mine and he frowns, shaking his head as he picks up my crutches and stands. "You don't have to go."

I break eye contact because if I keep looking at his gorgeous blue eyes, I will stay. "I think I've had enough excitement for tonight. It's time for me to go."

Mateo hands over my crutches and I hook them over my forearms and rise to my feet. I avoid touching him and smile at Max. "Can you take me to the lobby so that I can hail a cab?"

"I can take you," Mateo offers but I shake my head.

"I think I've kept you from Anne long enough." It's a borderline shitty thing to say and I know but I'm in full-on retreat mode and with the way he's looking at me, I'm not sure he'll just let me go. "It was good to see you Mateo. Thanks again."

He gives me a significant look but he goes, leaving me behind with Max who doesn't look like he's buying any of it.

"Just don't." I hold up my hand when he opens his mouth. "I can't talk about it. I'm all talked out."

"How do you know what I'm going to ask?"

I give him the same look Mateo just gave me. "It's what I would ask."

He nods. "Fair enough but if you need to talk... "

"I'll call Kit."

He laughs and offers his arm to me as we head to the elevators. "I like having you back in Nashville Carlisle Queen. I hope you decide to stay awhile."

"We'll see," is all I can answer.

Chapter Twenty-Seven

Mateo

"I thought you were staying with Anne," Zane says as I walk through the door at three in the morning.

I throw my keys on the table behind the sofa and walk to the fridge, opening it and snagging a beer from the shelf. I pop the top on the edge of the countertop and walk back to the couch where Zane is sitting and ease myself back on the cushions.

"What? You didn't bring one for me?" he asks, his hands open wide in the universal signal for "what-the-fuck-one-way"?

I flip him the bird and take a sip of my beer, dodging the pillow he throws at my face when he gets up to get his own beverage.

"If you're this much of an asshole, I bet Anne threw you out."

"I broke up with her," I say and take another sip while staring at the scuffed top of the coffee table we got for ten bucks at Goodwill the first week of sophomore year, when we moved out of the dorms and into our first apartment. "This table is a piece of shit, Zane. We should get a new one. You're working now, buy us a new fucking table."

He sits down next to me and places his feet on the table in question. "I like this table. I had my first three-way on this table."

"Sentimental value for the win," I say and chug back the rest of the bottle.

Zane hands me his beer.

"I kissed Carlisle at the party so I broke up with Anne."

"Do you want to kiss Carlisle again?" he asks.

I nod. "More than I want to do anything else on the planet."

"Well, then breaking up with Anne was the right thing to do." I shift to look at him and he examines me, his expression twisted with his confusion. "What? What's going on?"

"I don't know if I can be with Carlisle. We've got a terrible track record, so much shit under the bridge."

"You guys weren't together long enough to have a track record. It will be like starting new." He shrugs. "It's probably better to start new."

"Just let all that shit go? Act like it never happened?" I lean back on the sofa and stare at the ceiling. The dart we threw up there about a year ago is still wedged in the drywall. "A fresh start."

"Brand new except that you two crazy kids are already in love. You never stopped. I know it. You know it. Max knows it. The only one who didn't know it was Anne."

"Well thanks for making me feel like a bigger dick," I grumble and pick at the label on my beer bottle. "I didn't mean to hurt her. I thought Carlisle and I were done."

He shakes his head and laughs. "You two are never going to be done. You've got epic love song written all over you. Trust me, I know it when I see it."

"I need to talk to her. She was talking about leaving Nashville." I reach for my phone and slide the screen to access my contacts, too late remembering that the number I had for Carlisle was disconnected when she left. "Fuck, I'll have to ask Kit for her number tomorrow and then figure out where to find Carlisle."

It blows my mind that I don't know where the person I love most in the world actually lives.

"I have her number and I also know where she'll be tomorrow," Zane says with a grin on his face that says I'm going to pay for the information.

I groan but I know that whatever the price, I'll pay it.

"I'm not wearing a dress or eating anything alive," I warn him and groan when all he does is laugh.

Chapter Twenty-Eight

Mateo

I've never seen Carlisle swim in person, only on TV.

I walk into the competition size pool at the University and nod at the lifeguard watching her closely as she shoots through the water like a bullet. Her long and lithe body moves in one flawlessly executed movement and the sheer power of it takes my breath away.

"She's amazing isn't she," the man standing next me says as she dives under the surface and executes a perfect flip turn. "She was born to be in the water."

"She's so fast," I say and I know my voice is full of awe.

The guy chuckles beside me and glances down at the stopwatch he's holding. "Not fast enough for her, I'm afraid."

"Is she tough on herself?"

"I won't be able to get word in edgewise with the ass chewing she'll deliver to the girl in the mirror." He picks up a clipboard and writes down something on the sheet and smiles. "Easiest coaching job I've ever had. So much talent and drive. I almost don't need to be here."

Carlisle stops swimming and looks over at us, her eyes flaring wide with surprise at my presence. I wave and she waves back, a slight smile lifting her lips. She glides through the water, grips the edge and hauls herself out. A wheelchair is just behind her and I step forward to go help her but the guy next to puts a hand on my arm, stopping my progress.

"Unless you want to pull back a bloody stump, you need to let her do it. She'll ask for help if she needs it."

I stay where I am and watch her movements as she rolls the chair to her, sets the brake and lifts herself into the seat. She rolls over to a bench and removes her swim cap and grabs a towel, throwing it over her shoulders before joining us. She smiles at me but her focus is on her coach.

"How did I do, Joe?"

"You need to shave fifteen seconds off your time," he looks at me and grins when she mutters "fuck" under her breath, "And you need to work on keeping your hips from dipping down too low. It gives you too much drag. Use your weight work to strengthen your core and it should help a lot."

She nods and if the fierce determination on her face is any indication, she'll make it happen.

"Got it." Done with business, Carlisle makes the introductions. "Joe Griggs this is Mateo Butler."

We shake hands and then he moves off to gather their practice stuff.

"What are you training for?" I ask, suddenly nervous about my real reason to be there.

"I'm going to compete in the next Paralympics." She's running the towel over her body and squeezing the excess water out of her hair and delivers the news that she is going to compete on an international level again like it's something we all do.

"You've got a long way to go," Joe replies.

"And every time you tell me that, I am more and more determined to tell you to kiss my ass." She punctuates her words with a directly aimed glare.

I laugh at the exchange, enjoying the play between the two of them, the pink of her cheeks. Her eyes are like emerald fire and I know it's the joy of competing.

"I think you'll make it," I offer and she turns to Joe and gives him an "I told you so" look before returning back to me.

We stare at each other for a few minutes and I can see the big question of why I am here hanging over both of us.

I take a deep breath and decide to jump in with both feet. "I broke up with Anne."

She pauses, her lips parting on a silent "oh" at my disclosure.

"I'm sorry for that," she whispers, "She seemed to be a very nice person."

"She was and she deserved more than what I could give her. So I ended it."

My words fall into the silence as I watch Carlisle and she looks everywhere but at me. Her fingers twist the towel in her hands, the biggest clue that she's as nervous as I am.

I decide to put us both out of our misery.

"I was running errands today and you were on my list."

Her eyes snap to meet mine and her cheeks flush bright pink with her surprise. I can see her pulse pounding on her throat and she swallows before she answers.

"At least I made the list." Her lips twitch with the hint of a smile and it gives me the guts to continue.

"You were first on the list but I was trying to get the nerve to come see you." And then I keep going. "I wanted to see if you wanted to go out with me sometime. On a date." I press my luck when her smile gets wider. "If you have time for a coffee now, I can wait."

"Will my wheelchair fit in your trunk? I got a ride from Joe, so I'll need one home."

"I'll make room."

***

The coffee house down the street from the University aquatic center is crowded and we opt for a table outside on the patio where it is quiet and almost deserted. Dusk has settled on the city and it's a little chilly in the air but the outdoor space heater and my excitement over being here with Carlisle keeps it at bay.

I come back to the table with our drinks and a couple of brownies and I settle into the chair next her wheelchair. I should probably give her some space but I don't know if I can stand to be even a table-length away from her. She doesn't seem to mind since she's leaning towards me, our arms brushing against each other as we move.

We both take a sip of our drinks but before it has a chance to get weird, I jump in.

"It was really great to see you swimming again."

She brushes a stray curl off her face and tucks it behind her ear and my fingers itch to do that for her. I grip my coffee tighter in an effort to keep them to myself.

"At the rehab place in Texas they really pushed me to get in the pool. Once I realized how much it helped my progress you couldn't keep me out of it."

"And the Paralympics?"

"That was me, being me. If there is someone to beat, I'm on it." She shrugs her shoulders. "Time will tell if I'll be successful or not."

"If I know you, you'll dominate the field as usual." She shrugs again and we stare at each other for several long moments before she begins, never breaking eye contact with me. I have no desire to look anywhere but at her so I'm good with it.

"And what about you and medical school?" She reaches over and touches my hand, letting her touch linger before she returns it to her cup. "Max and Kit told me you're doing great."

"I love it. It's hard and I'm tired all the time but I'm glad I went." I bump her with my shoulder and give credit where credit is due. "I'm glad you convinced me to go. I love working in the free clinic and I'm already planning to go into the General Practice track."

"So the Butler family practice will be a reality then?" she asks.

"I'm sure Mari is happy up there looking down on her big brother." I need to touch her so I reach over and take her hand, holding it between us. "Is this okay? I just can't sit next to you and not touch you."

"It's more than okay," she whispers and I lean over, brushing our lips against each other. Soft and gentle, the hint of coffee on our lips. I pull back and her eyes are closed so I move in again and take another until she sighs. "People are probably watching us."

"They're just jealous."

She laughs and moves away, just a little, enough for us to look at each other as we talk.

"How often are you in the wheelchair?"

"It depends on so many things. I use it far less than the crutches but if I have been on my feet a lot or if I my body decides to boycott, I'm usually in for a day or two. I've learned to read my body and the signals and I can stay out of it if I respect my limits and keep up my exercise."

"Do you still feel like you made the right decision?" I ask and I hold my breath not sure I'm ready to hear the answer. She seems to be happy but I know how hard the early days were for her and how much she doubted her choice.

"Yes, I do. It's not easy all the time but it's worth it." Her gaze is clear and sure. "I made the right call, I'm just sorry that I didn't know it soon enough to avoid hurting you."

And here we are at the crossroads and I know where I want to go. I just need to know if she is with me.

"Carlisle I understand better how it all went to hell. It's in the past and we are here now and I don't want to waste time going over and over what we could have done differently or better or whatever. I just want you."

"I want you too." She hesitates, her eyes cloudy with the uncertainty our past put there and I regret it. "Do you think we can just start over?"

"I don't want to start over. I want to begin again. Brand new as the people we are now, living with the choices we made in the past and choosing to be here together now."

A tear hovers on her lashes and splashes down her cheek and I lean forward, kissing it away.

"I'm not the same woman I was before Mateo. My body…"

"Carlisle, you can tell me anything. If we are going to be together we have to be honest with each other, shares our worries and our fears. I don't want what we had before, I want all of you sharing everything with me and I will do the same."

I think I know what she's worried about, the physical side of us after her injury. I've done my research and I'm sure

I know what to expect but I want her to confide in me, to share. It's a huge step and the tightness in my chest releases when she takes it.

"My body needs help to function. It's getting better and the doctors think that I will eventually get beyond needing the assistance but I have to use enemas and catheters to maintain my health. Sex is completely on the table and I want it but I need help with lube and extra stimulation to have an orgasm. It's not a lot in my opinion but for some guys it might be too much. I don't know if it's too much for you."

Her hands are lying flat on the table in between us and it is the most natural thing in the world for me to put my hands in them and hold on tight.

"Carlisle, when I came back to you the night I found out about the surgery it was because it is impossible for me to be without you. I decided before I even got in the car that it didn't matter how it turned out, I was prepared to be by your side until one of takes our last breath. None of that has changed in all this time and it never will. It will never matter to me if you are on your own two feet or in a wheelchair or if we have to buy out the adult toy store and a lube factory to make sure you have everything you want and need in bed. I love you, *Tesoro* and you are perfect to me."

She's crying full-on now and I release her hands to cup her face and kiss away the tears. Her eyelashes, her cheeks, and finally her mouth. Sweet, drugging kisses that leave both of us breathless and laughing.

"I love you, Teo."

And once again, that's all I need to hear.

Chapter Twenty-Nine

Mateo

I haven't been this nervous on a date since I was a teenager.

Carlisle's new place is really nice. The twenty-four hour guard had my name at the front desk and buzzed me into the elevator that shot straight to her floor. I clutch my gifts in my hands and second-guess myself yet another time. I think what I brought is okay considering the step we took yesterday and I hope it will help us have a new beginning. New memories. New understanding. New commitment.

The elevator doors open and I am facing the long hallway. I swallow down the nerves fluttering around in my belly and take one step and then the next until I find myself at her door. I press the button and wait. The lock turns, the handle moves, and the door sweeps open.

At first I see no one and then I look down. Carlisle looks up at me from her wheelchair and the smile she gives me is tentative, her eyes questioning.

"It's a wheelchair day," I observe, using her own words and I relax when relief crosses her features and her eyes sparkle. She wasn't sure how I would react and that makes my heart hurt a little.

We might have come so far but we still have a ways to go. Mateo and Carlisle are still a work-in-progress.

"I had a fundraiser this morning and I walked a lot. My legs are a little tired," she explains and then, "Come on in. Dinner is keeping warm in the oven. I hope you like lasagna," she says as she maneuvers her chair through the entryway and into her place. The living room is floor-to-ceiling windows and we've got the Nashville skyline lit up like a Christmas at our feet. I stop and stare.

"Oh my God. This is gorgeous." I look over at her and smile. "Quite a change from your last place. You stopped slumming."

She tosses her hair back over her shoulder and makes a face. "You sound like Livvy."

"And she's right." I hand her one of the packages I have in my hand. "A housewarming gift."

"You didn't have to but since I love presents, I'll take it." She snatches it out of my hand wheels over to the living space, motioning for me to take a seat next to her. The way she has her sofa arranged, with one side armless she can roll her chair up and its like we're sitting side-by-side.

I lower myself to the cushions and watch her as she rips off the paper. I know what's inside the wrapping paper, so I focus on her. The way her emerald eyes are glowing, her red-gold hair longer and draped around her shoulders like a veil. Yesterday when we kissed, the caress of it's silk on my skin was luxurious.

"You're gorgeous," I blurt out and she stops what's she's doing, meeting my eyes.

"What?"

"You're just the most fucking beautiful thing I have ever seen in my whole life and I can't stop looking at you." I grin, unapologetic in my adoration.

I could play it cool but I'm not. She's the one for me. I know it. She knows it.

"Teo... "

"Open your present," I urge and she watches me for a few seconds before looking back down and pulling off the rest of the wrapping paper.

She stares at it for a moment, confusion on her features and then her face lights up. She smiles as she runs her fingers over the framed t-shirt.

"It's from the concert... our first 'non date'."

"I bought it and forgot to give it to you. I kept it so... " I feel kind of stupid now that I've given it to her. "I thought you might want it."

"I love it," she says and holds it to her chest, her smile genuine. "That is an excellent memory."

"Yeah the show was great."

"I wasn't talking about the show," she says and my body reacts to the sultry lilt to her words.

We stare at each other. There's so much electricity pulsing between us that I fully expect the appliances in her kitchen to short out. I lean over and she leans in, the first brush of our mouths sparking with static. We pull back and look each other, laughing.

"I've never laughed with anyone like I do with you," I murmur, zooming back in for a new press of our lips.

She's still smiling when our lips meet and when I press forward to part her lips with my tongue, it is effortless. Natural. It's like there was never a gap.

I feel her hand reach out to grab my shirt and pull me closer, she tilts her head so I can have better access to her mouth. I take what she is offering to me, indulging my need to reconnect with her this way with sweeps of my tongue, nibbles on her lips.

I pull back and make eye contact with her, leaning forward to hook my arm under her legs and she loops her arms around my neck. I position her in my lap, the full body contact intensifying the kisses when I lean back in for more.

We make out on the couch like teenagers. Hands roaming over clothes at first and then she starts unbuttoning my shirt and caressing my chest with her cool fingers. I caress her back, rubbing circles downward until I each the hem of her blouse and burrow underneath, coasting my palm against the silken skin. The bra strap interrupts my journey so I open the clasp and expose her entire back to my exploration.

She's thinner but more muscular and I love the play of her muscles underneath my touch. Carlisle is raking her fingernails against my chest, over my nipples and I groan, releasing her from the kiss as I run my mouth over the place where her shirt has slipped off. A bite to the place where her shoulder meets her neck and she's gasping. Soft pants of desire against my hair as I continue my tasting tour along the column of her neck.

"You are perfect. A dream," I whisper when I reach the tender shell of her ear.

Carlisle reaches around and grabs my hand under her shirt and I pull back, thinking she is going to move it away but instead she drags it to the front and places it on her breast. I look up and meet her eyes, making sure we're on the same page.

"Mateo, touch me please. It's been too long," she whispers against my mouth, her tongue tracing my bottom lip before she dives in for another kiss.

I move my hand upward and cup the heavy weight of her breast in my palm. Skimming my thumb lightly over her nipple. Carlisle's fingernails dig into my bicep, my back, as she arches into my touch, begging me for more.

I want to give her whatever she wants but not on this couch.

"I'm not going to do this for the first time on your sofa. May I take you to bed?" I ask, staring down at her so that I can see every nuance of emotion on her face. "I know this is fast. We don't… "

"I want to try this with you, Teo. I want you in my bed and in my life. Please."

She doesn't have to ask me twice. I adjust my grip on her body and stand, at the last minute remembering my other gift. "Lean over and grab that please."

She does as I ask, her eyebrows drawn together in confusion. "What's this?"

"Something to help us navigate this new beginning."

"You bought me a GPS?" She teases and I grin back. Laughter and sex and Carlisle always seem to go together for me.

"In a way. You'll see."

I walk into the bedroom stopping just over the threshold to look around. It's a large room with the bold splashes of color on a dove gray background. The bed is set along one wall, the floor-to-ceiling windows covering another, a bathroom and closet taking up the rest of the space. I stare at the bed, doubt that this is the right time clouds my mind.

Carlisle's fingertips under my chin guide my gaze back to her own. It's like she can read my mind because she smiles at me and assures me, "I want this Mateo."

"Is there anything you need to do before we do this Carlisle? Can I help you?" I don't know how she'll react to my question; don't know if it will kill the mood blooming between us.

She shakes her head. "Not tonight. I took care of it earlier but I might need help later."

Her admission makes my chest hurt. I know how hard it is for her to ask for help, it was one of the things that brought us down before. But we both want this to work, we want to be together and that requires us to be different. To begin now.

I lower her to the bed and step back, watching her as I slowly unbutton the rest of my shirt. She leans back on her elbows, ogling me with a sexy, mischievous smile on her lips

"I like the view," she says, reaching over her head to grab the back of her shirt and pull it off, tossing it to the floor. I mimic her behavior and she leers with a sexy grin. "Keep going. It gets better and better by the minute."

"Pevert."

"But I'm *your* pervert," she says and throws off her bra.

That stops me with my jeans unbuttoned, my fly undone. I stare and then drop to my knees at her feet, diving in to take one of her rose-colored nipples in my mouth.

"You have gorgeous tits. I have always loved your tits," I mumble as I trace a path of kisses across her collarbone and take the other one in my mouth for lavish attention.

Carlisle's fingers are in my hair, holding me in place as I devour her. She starts the panting, the moaning that haunted my dreams for ten months. I'm so hard for her that I jump when her hand drops to my crotch and inserts itself inside my jeans to stroke me. I throw my head back enjoying the sensation, thrusting into her grip as my blood heats up.

It feels good and I want it continue but this first time has to be more about her than me. I need to show her that although we might have to find new ways of enjoying each other, we will still be combustible in bed. I need to show her that she is enough and will always be for me.

I pull back and move her hand away. "Get undressed. I want to make you feel good."

I shuck off my jeans and watch as she removes her skirt and them scoots back on the bed until she is naked and fully open to me in the middle. I reach down and open the package that I brought with me, handing the contents over to her with a smile.

"You told me that we might have to be creative and I took you at your word."

***

Carlisle

I look down at what Mateo has placed in my hand and try to figure out what it is.

A wrist band, similar to the kind you use to strap your iPod to your arm when you run. From it's black material emerges two wires that lead to a set of pads that fit over the fingertips.

"Here let me show you," Mateo says, kneeling naked next me on the bed, his body distracting me from what he's doing. Ten months has not changed him at all. Skin still tan, hair dark, muscles everywhere a man is supposed to have them. If I wasn't really curious about what he brought me, I'd be exploring him up close and personal right now.

He fastens the wristband over his wrist and slips the pads over his fingers and presses a button on the band. A slight vibration sound fills the air between us and he reaches out to cup my breast.

"How does this feel?" He asks as he lightly runs his fingers over my skin. I react immediately, goosebumps running up and down my skin and then a jolt of electricity that runs straight to my sex when he glances it over a nipple.

"Holy hell," I gasp and clutch at his shoulder when he

makes another pass at my nipple. "That's amazing."

"Can you feel it? I know you said that you needed more pressure more intense sensation. Is this enough?"

I open my eyes and look at the blue eyes of the most generous lover, the most perfect partner anybody could ask for.

"It's amazing," I say and cup his face in my hands, pressing our foreheads together, a replica of what he does that drives me crazy. "And *you* are amazing. I love you Mateo."

"I love you too. I'll do anything for you, *Tesoro*. All you have to do is ask."

"Come here and fuck me, Teo. It's been too long." I lean back on the bed and shift my legs, spreading them for him in invitation. I worry briefly that the heaviness in my limbs makes my movement more awkward than sexy but one look at Mateo's face erases that doubt from my mind. He's hungry for me and I can't wait for him to eat me up.

Mateo crawls up between my legs, leaning over to kiss me. Slow kisses, with deep tongue and tender nips that build our passion again. I run my hands over his back, down his chest, stroking his cock and reveling in the way his hips buck into my palm. He's leaking pre-come and it makes the glides slicker, my thumb rubbed over his head makes his whole body jump and we laugh softly.

"Two can play at that game," he growls against the sensitive skin just below my ear before he travels down my body. He presses soft kisses on my breasts, soft licks against nipples that make me squirm with the jolts of pleasure that shoot to my sex. I'm aroused, to a point more intense than where I've gotten on my own and watching Teo kissing down my belly spikes it even higher. I push the worry to the back of mind and just enjoy every moment with my lover.

He gives me one long look from his place between my legs before he dips his head and gives my entire sex a long lick that ends with a swirl on my clit. I arch off the bed a little, surprised by the amount of sensation I am feeling from such a gentle touch.

"Feel good?" He asks and when I nod he smirks. "Let's see how this is for you."

And then the pad on one of his fingers joins his mouth and I'm clutching at my comforter, twisting it in my grip as I cry out. Mateo groans and I reach down to cup the back of his head. It's intense, powerful and delicious. I'm too busy reveling in it to compare it whatever it was like before.

"Oh my God, don't stop. Please."

I look down to enjoy the view of this man pleasuring me with his mouth, His dark, sleek body writhing as he grinds his cock against the bed as I fuck up into his mouth. Its heaven and hell and I don't want to be anywhere else right now. An orgasm is building and I strain to reach it, a frustrated moan escaping my lips.

"Play with your nipples. Get your fingers real wet and play with them for me. I'll get you there Carlisle."

Mateo's eyes are a dark navy as he watches me follow his directions. Two fingers in my mouth, spit slick and twisting the sensitive tips before he finally resumes eating me out. He never takes his eyes off me and his eyes are the last things I see before I close my eyes when I come.

Fireworks. Shooting stars. An entire universe exploding behind my eyelids as I writhe against his mouth, against the vibrator before I even start to float back to Earth.

He crawls up my body, taking off the vibrator and setting it to side of us on the bed before he leans down and kisses me. Thorough. Wet. Deep. Passionate. I throw my arms around his neck, keeping him close, pulling him down on top of me, relishing the weight of him on me, my taste in his mouth.

"Was it good?" he asks, his worry plain in the tone of his voice.

I grasp his face and force him to look at me. "It was amazing. Perfect."

"Thank God," he breathes and lowers his forehead to mine, his nose rubbing mine before leaning down to kiss me again.

"I want you inside of me, Teo. Please." I realize that I am going to have to ask, to guide him this time. New territory for both and too much opportunity to misstep if we aren't honest with one another. I nod when he asks if I am sure.

He turns and picks up the tube of lube from my side table and offers it to me.

"Get me ready, baby."

I take it and pour some in my palm, sliding it over his cock and enjoying the hiss and groans my touch pulls out of him. When he's slick enough, he settles in between my legs and pushes inside me.

I gasp at the fullness, the pressure that settles in my body when he is deep inside me. I've missed this. So much. I blink back the tears that in my eyes but I'm too late. Several roll down my face and Mateo stills. He watches me, waiting for my signal, his gaze patient and open. I can see the love pouring off him, the desire he has to make me happy.

"Are you okay?" He asks and I nod and he leans down, kissing me softly. "Good tears?"

"Yes," I whisper the word and it turns a moan when he moves deeper inside me.

We take it slow. This is not the time for hard and fast. We don't want to rush but the need for the physical connection has us both shaking. He pushes inside and I lift to meet each of his thrusts, the pressure creating a warm, sensual warmth rushing over my skin. I reach over and pull the vibrator to me, placing it on my hand like I saw him do it and I turn it on.

I run my hand over my collarbone, down between my breasts, across my belly, awakening the nerve endings under my skin. Mateo watches the entire time, his eyes tracking the path, a soft curse escaping his mouth when I detour back up to my nipples. The stimulation is direct, strong and Mateo stutters his strokes when my sex clenches around him.

"*Tesoro*," he says, his voice full of desire, want, and love. "I'm getting close. You feel too damn good."

"Come on Teo," I lift my head to capture his mouth in

a carnal kiss that has his hips speeding up as he thrusts into me. He reaches down and grasps my legs, lifting them and opening me to him completely and he takes what he needs. I reach down between us and touch my clit with the finger pad and when he goes still above me with his release, a gentler orgasm from the one I had earlier races through my system.

Teo lowers himself to lie beside me, pulling me against his body as the little spoon to his larger one. I fit tight against him, the top of my head wedged underneath his chin, his arm lying possessively over my waist. We stare out of the windows, watching the lights of Nashville below us.

"*Tesoro*," Mateo says, his voice low and dark and tinged with the gravel of emotion. Soft kisses across my jaw, against my temple, my bare shoulder. "You *are* my treasure, you know."

I roll over to face him, the lights below nothing compared to his face. Nothing compared to his love.

"Teo, I have had fame and fortune. *Solo te necesito a ti.*" And it is true. All I need is him.

He smiles, leaning down to kiss my but veers off at the last, shaking his head. "Your accent is really terrible."

I grin back. "We've got lots of time for you to help me practice.

"Yes, we do."

Epilogue

Carlisle

Four months later.

I never thought I would be here again.

I am standing on the block at the start of my first race at the Paralympics games. The stands are full of people and the press area is bursting with reporters anxious to get a shot of me as I compete again for the first time since the bombing. I am now, and I love it, an ambassador and spokesperson for disabled people and athletes around the world. It is fulfilling work and it takes the focus off the tragedy of that day and gives back a little hope because I, and all the other survivors, are proving that they could not destroy us.

And even though Aaron is gone, he lives on in his foundation and the good it is doing. There are several athletes here who trained and traveled with a grant from our fundraising efforts and I couldn't be more proud. I turned the day-to-day running of it to his parents and we are growing closer everyday. We spend more time laughing at memories of him than crying. It's a good thing.

I stare at the water below me. Blue, sparkling and probably too cool and I cannot wait to get in it. I am in the pool everyday as I push myself to do better, to be better. Today is the result of all my hard work and whether I take home another medal or if I just finish this heat, it will be worth it.

I look up in the stands and I find my parents and the Butlers waving to me. My mom has her knitting needles in her hand and an unfinished blanket on her lap as usual. Livvy and Sarah are here too and my best friend gives me the thumbs up when I catch her eye.

And there is Teo. My rock. My best friend. My love. I

think we're getting it right this time. I lean on him more and he doesn't try to protect me from everything. We work. It isn't flawless but it is real.

He doesn't know it but I'm going to ask him to move in with me after the games are over. From the way he's smiling at me right now, I think he'll say yes.

Another step for us. Another new beginning.

The buzzer goes off signaling one minute until the race starts so I tear my gaze away from him and focus. I get into position, take a few deep breaths and close my eyes. Everything goes away except my heartbeat and the call of the water.

I take another deep breath.

The buzzer goes off.

I open my eyes and jump.

If you loved **SALVATION**, continue with the rest of the Nashville Nights series...

TEMPTATION

She needs to be good.

At sixteen, Kit ditched her crappy life and moved to Nashville with only $200, her guitar, and a notebook full of songs. She hit it big, but five years of living like a rock star plus a stint in rehab has killed any good will she had with her label. The suits have ordered Kit to shape up or ship out of the limelight. The last thing she needs is a hot, sexy distraction with a sinful smile.

He doesn't know the meaning of the word.

Max Butler is as far from a celebrity as you can get and he likes it that way. A Nashville firefighter, he's living the single life with a revolving door of parties, friends, and a different woman in his bed every night. When his normal life suddenly collides with the girl on his favorite Rolling Stone cover, he sees the perfect chance to fulfill his ultimate fantasy and see just how bad Kit can be.

Sometimes bad is so very good.

With three weeks until Kit leaves for her big tour, Max promises to give her a break from being the good girl--no strings attached. But when hot days lead to sultry nights, the lines get blurred and suddenly three weeks of bad might not be good enough.

Buy it on the TEMPTATION page.

REDEMPTION

Holding on never felt so good.

Emory Cabell is leaving the lies behind her.

Finding out that you're the half-sister to America's country music queen is game changer. Determined to meet the sibling she never knew and compelled to pursue the music career she's always wanted, Emory leaves her small town and heads to Nashville. Thrown by the bustle of Music City and the cutthroat dealing of the business, she finds unexpected shelter in a musical partnership with country music's notorious bad boy.

Zane has his eyes set on the prize.

Known as a man who never stays the night, Zane is reliable only when it comes to his music. Years of paying his dues has gained him the coveted lead guitarist spot on the hottest music tour of the year. Hoping this gig will lead to his own recording contract, he agrees to write a few songs with Emory but he's blown away by the sexual chemistry sizzling between them and leveled by his feelings for this quiet woman with the beautiful soul.

Can love be more than just a line in a song?

Darkness and light... they should not work. But one night in her bed proves they're hotter than the number one single they wrote together. Things get complicated when the spotlight sheds light on all of Zane's past sins and Emory struggles with trusting him with her heart. When the sought after recording contract stipulates they remain a duet, it threatens everything Zane has worked towards and challenges everything he thought he knew about himself. With his life at a crossroads, will he choose the music or the future with a woman whose love might just be his redemption?

Buy it on the REDEMPTION page.

ACKNOWLEDGMENTS

Huge, huge thanks to everyone who helped me get this book in your hands.

My best friends, Avery Flynn and Kimberly Kincaid, for keeping me on track and kicking my ass when necessary.

My editor, Nicole, for putting up with my crazy.

For Meredith and Anessa formatting — you always make it look so pretty!

For the Sizzlemongers... I couldn't ask for a better group of friends. Not just a street team, we have become a group who support each other and I love that so hard.

Nancy Weeks — thank you for opening up your story and your heart to me. I cherish your friendship. XXX

The Main Man, Little Man and Lulu. My reasons to keep going, you are the fulfillment of a dream I didn't even know I had. I am a very lucky woman.

Dear Reader —

Thanks so much for reading my book. If you enjoyed this novella you can find out latest info on my next release and enter for the monthly giveaway by signing up for my newsletter. You can also drop me a line at robin@robincovingtonromance.com. I'd love to hear from you.

And if you are so inclined, please leave a review on Amazon, Barnes & Noble, iBooks, or Goodreads.

I love to explore the theme of fooling around and falling in love in my books and I adore a hero who falls hard. When I'm not writing sexy, sizzling romance, I collect tasty man candy pics, indulge in a little comic book geek love, collect red nail polish, and obsess over Dean Winchester. Don't send chocolate… send eye-candy!

There are so many great books out there and I'm grateful that you spent your money and time to read my book.

Xx,
Robin

****

Social Media Links:

Website: www.robincovingtonromance.com
Facebook Profile: http://on.fb.me/YSW9n3
Facebook Page: http://on.fb.me/1fCyWuQ
Twitter: @RobinCovington
Pinterest: http://bit.ly/1c1Tm5u
Newsletter sign up: http://eepurl.com/qjFcz

If you enjoyed SALVATION, check out my other books:

A NIGHT OF SOUTHERN COMFORT

HIS SOUTHERN TEMPTATION

SWEET SOUTHERN BETRAYAL

PLAYING THE PART

SEX & THE SINGLE VAMP

PLAYING WITH THE DRUMMER

DARING THE PLAYER

TEMPTATION

SECRET SANTA BABY

www.ingramcontent.com/pod-product-compliance
Lightning Source LLC
Chambersburg PA
CBHW060146130626
46556CB00006B/2510